Between
HEAVEN
and EARTH

Between HEAVEN and EARTH

A STORY OF NINETEENTH-CENTURY JERUSALEM

Sue Kerman

gefen publishing house גפן בית הוצאה לאור Est. 1981
JERUSALEM • NEW YORK

Cover Design and Typesetting by S. Kim Glassman

ISBN: 978-965-229-516-3

1 3 5 7 9 8 6 4 2

Gefen Publishing House, Ltd.
6 Hatzvi Street
Jerusalem 94386, Israel
972-2-538-0247
orders@gefenpublishing.com

Gefen Books
11 Edison Place
Springfield, NJ 07081, USA
1-800-477-5257
orders@gefenpublishing.com

www.gefenpublishing.com

Printed in Israel   *Send for our free catalogue*

Library of Congress Cataloging-in-Publication Data

Kerman, Sue.
Between heaven and earth : a story of nineteenth-century Jerusalem /
Sue Kerman.
p. cm.
Includes bibliographical references.
ISBN 978-965-229-516-3 (alk. paper)
I. Title.
PR9510.9.K36B48 2011
823'.92--dc23

To my wonderful nephews and nieces
and their families.

Contents

PART II

PART III

PART IV

PART V

PART VI

EPILOGUE

Acknowledgments

Special thanks to
Diane Greenberg, Caren Neuman and Evan Fallenberg
for their advice and encouragement.

And to
Amnon Ramon of Yad Ben Zvi,
who introduced me to this fascinating period
in Jerusalem's history.

Introduction

David looked up and saw the angel of the Lord standing between heaven and earth, with a drawn sword in his hand extended over Jerusalem.

1 Chronicles 21:16

Jerusalem was not a religious city from birth. David did not build his city in a place that had strategic or economic significance. It was not even on the main road. An early story tells of a man making a journey with his wife from the north of the country to Hebron. He decided not to stop in Jerusalem for the night because it was too far off the beaten track.

David conquered the Jebusite fortress of Jerusalem and built his capital on those empty hills for political reasons, because the town was neutral. It did not belong to any of the twelve tribes. He brought the Ark of the Covenant there, intending to build a temple, but God said that it must wait for a later generation.

Jerusalem only took on a religious patina with time. Only when the city had acquired political and religious stature was it recalled that Abraham had wandered in the area, and that he had almost sacrificed his son Isaac, probably on Mount Moriah.

Like an old brass pot, Jerusalem has been passed from owner to owner, sometimes cared for, sometimes neglected, sometimes battered and sometimes restored, sometimes polished up to shine brightly and sometimes left to lose its luster.

PART I

Chapter 1

Rebecca's Inheritance

Rebecca Silver suddenly found herself at loose ends – thirty-five years old with no real ballast to hold her down. The catalog for the exhibit of early twentieth-century Russian avant-garde art which she had been slaving over for the last year and a half had been completed in eerie coincidence with the finalization of her divorce papers. So here she was – no husband, no job. And no children – her most poignant regret.

She was also homeless, as she and Warren had amicably agreed to sell their Brooklyn apartment and split the proceeds. Despite everything, she was going to miss him and miss being married to him. Their separation had been due more to their naïveté about the minutiae of married life than to any irreconcilable differences.

Then, suddenly, her grandmother had died last month – that tiny, vital woman who, when Rebecca's parents had suddenly been killed, had filled the vast chasm in Rebecca's life with her strong, grounded presence. Her only meaningful family tie severed over-night. All she had left of her grandmother now were a few souvenirs. A jade pendant Gran had bought her on a visit to San Francisco, which Rebecca had put on the day of the funeral and hadn't taken off since. A Matisse print she had always coveted, which would probably now be stuck away in storage for a good long while. A book of Rilke's poetry that had belonged to her mother. And an aged female Labrador named Elsie, whom she knew would have to be put down. Another loss.

But there was one more legacy. Several boxes filled with letters, photos, yellowing newspaper clippings and dozens of journals left behind about 150 years ago which had belonged to some great-great-aunt of her grandfather.

Strangely enough, her grandmother had shared with her the scant information she had about the woman when she handed the boxes over to her a week before her death. The two of them were sitting in the kitchen of Gran's dimly lit apartment on the Upper East Side.

Rebecca's paternal grandparents had lived in this rent-controlled apartment on Eighty-eighth and Lexington since the fifties, when her grandfather was transferred from the Midwest by the insurance company he worked for. Gran had never gotten used to the frenetic pace of life in the city. For all the years she lived there she had avoided going outside at rush hour, afraid she would be "whooshed" down the street against her will to some unknown destination by the force of inertia. In the past few years she seldom went outside at all, protecting her brittle bones from the accidental assault of any unthinking New Yorker who considered reaching his destination on time more important than the welfare of a fragile old woman. Rebecca had inherited Gran's slight build as well as her aversion to the city. Her parents, on the other hand, had loved the buzz of their high-powered jobs in the financial sector and Rebecca – unjustly, Gran maintained – blamed their lifestyle for their deaths and for her being left alone at such an early age. Rebecca promised herself to settle down in a much more tranquil locale some day.

It was in this apartment that Gran had brought up Rebecca's father, Richard. And when he got married and moved out to Park Slope with Rebecca's mother and their baby daughter, he would bring his family into Manhattan for Sunday brunch. Rebecca's parents would leave her with her grandparents when they went off on one of their frequent vacations. And it was to here that Rebecca had moved permanently when her parents were killed in a plane crash in 1982 on their way to the Bahamas.

Gran's apartment was her real childhood home. Every time she walked into the modest lobby of the building and was greeted by Frank, the ubiquitous doorman who had been opening the door for her since she could remember – when she was younger with a playful pat on the head and as she matured with more and more reserve – she thought back to the secure years she had spent there.

She pondered in retrospect how Gran had dealt with the devastating loss of her ailing husband and a year later of her son and daughter-in-law, and had then found the courage to take care of her only grandchild. Just to make life more challenging, this very Anglo-Saxon grandmother with her tightly curled, salt-and-pepper hair and soft, delicate features would don her Scottish woolen sweater and her pleated tartan skirt, her daily uniform when she ventured out of her apartment, to volunteer at the 92nd Street Y teaching remedial reading to underprivileged children. This she did with the same fiery enthusiasm she applied to everything else.

The utilitarian furnishings of the apartment reflected Gran's no-nonsense personality. Aside from a few decorative Bargello cushions and a Bargello quilt thrown over the living room sofa that she had made herself, and the couple of prints on the walls – the Matisse that Rebecca had coveted and a sensuous picture of autumn leaves by Georgia O'Keefe bought at the Metropolitan, where she took Rebecca from time to time – as well as a few family photographs, the décor of Gran's apartment was plain and dark. The boxes were demonstratively positioned in the middle of the navy blue living room rug when Rebecca had come to visit for the last time.

She and her grandmother had sat at the wobbly wooden kitchen table over coffee and grilled cheese sandwiches, just as they had done when she was small and once a week for the past ten years or so, since Rebecca had returned to the city from her art studies in Boston. It was at this table that Gran had patiently passed on her life wisdom to Rebecca, through endless edifying stories about her family and the people she had known, many of which she herself had heard from her Scottish parents as a child in a small Midwestern town.

Rebecca had as usual burned her palate on the open cheese sandwich since Gran always grilled them with the tomatoes on top, "like a pizza," as she used to say encouragingly to Rebecca when she was younger. The conversation came around to the owner of the contents of the boxes, which it turned out had been taking up Gran's entire storage locker for the past twenty years.

"To tell you the truth, Rebecca" – Gran always prefaced her most significant remarks with "to tell you the truth," as if the rest of the time she had been propagating endless lies – "this woman is a complete conundrum to us all. The legend is that she went off to Jerusalem a short time after her husband died back in the mid-nineteenth century. Her children were grown up and married. She must have felt she had fulfilled her maternal duties and could spend some time on herself, although I'm sure that life in Jerusalem back then was no picnic. In any case, she corresponded with her family for a while but the letters became less and less frequent over the years until at one point they stopped coming altogether."

"Weren't you ever curious to sift through some of this stuff yourself?" Rebecca said, eyeing the boxes as she would a possibly rare, but suspiciously dubious, work of art.

"To tell you the truth, sweetheart," continued Gran, fussing with a loose thread on the corner of the tablecloth, "I never had the time. It was always one thing after another – bringing up your father, taking care of a dying husband, and then, when your parents were killed in that horrific accident, helping you get through that rough time, which you did so incredibly well, my dear," she added with a heartfelt smile, patting Rebecca's hand gently. "Your grandfather had no real connection to this woman. She must have died some time back at the end of the nineteenth century or early in the twentieth."

"How did these boxes end up here, anyway?" Rebecca asked as she shifted her right leg up under her trim bottom.

"A woman by the name of Elizabeth Finn – you can still see the Jerusalem address on the boxes – sent them on to your grandfather's family through a friend of hers and from there they were handed down from one generation to the next until they finally ended up here. We didn't know quite what to do with them, but we didn't have the heart to throw them out."

Gran stood up with difficulty, pushing down with both hands on the table, which groaned slightly under her weight. She slowly walked over to the boxes and leaned tentatively over one of them, the flesh hanging loosely from her flaccid arms as she pointed to the name and address printed on it in black ink. Rebecca remembered noticing at the time how frail Gran had become.

"You can see here, her name was Zara Rubens, and she was from your father's side of the family. And that's all I know." It took considerable effort for Gran to stand herself upright again before she continued. "I thought maybe now that you have some time on your hands you might be interested in looking over the contents of these boxes. I know you always had a partiality to your Jewish roots. And you were always so good at doing research when you were at college. In any case, do with them whatever you will. It's your problem now."

Rebecca thought back to that conversation on the day of the funeral. Gran must have had premonitions about her imminent demise the day she handed those boxes over to her. She also thought about the assumptions Gran had made about her in that short conversation. Now that Gran was dead, they whirled around in her head like an unsolved riddle.

That she had some time on her hands there was no doubt. She had oodles of time. As for her "partiality to her Jewish roots," well, she had never thought about it that much, although there were aspects of Judaism she wanted to explore. And as for her research skills, they had earned her the nickname of "the mole" at college because once she got stuck into a subject she would never let up until she had plumbed it to its depths.

Rebecca sat on the sole remaining kitchen chair in the middle of the living room of Gran's apartment, thoughtfully curling a strand of her long auburn hair around her index finger. She was surrounded by her suitcases, the Matisse and the boxes, with Elsie lying mournfully in the corner. There seemed to be nothing she could do to comfort the poor thing. She had sold off Gran's belongings to one of those bloodsuckers always willing to turn a quick profit on the remnants of another person's life. She was now going to move in with her friend Yana in Chelsea until she could figure out what to do with the rest of her life.

She glanced over at the boxes and found herself drawn to one of them. As Gran had said, the return address was written on it in bold, black letters: "Elizabeth Finn, Abraham's Vineyard, Jerusalem, Palestine." Looking from one to the other of the boxes, she saw "Zara Rubens's property" was written on eight of them, numbered in chronological order. There were three other boxes labeled "Letters to Helga" by someone else. She picked out a faded sepia photograph from the first of the Zara Rubens boxes. On the back was inscribed in a neat, unembellished handwriting, very different from the firm, no-nonsense block letters on the outside of the boxes: "The Finns and I, Jerusalem, 1856."

In the photo was a respectable couple with a somewhat confused-looking, shorter woman standing beside them. The deferential distance they maintained suggested they were not that familiar with each other, but from the warmth of their expressions, it looked like they were nevertheless enjoying each other's company.

The man had a balding pate, his few remaining hairs standing on end as if in shock at being left to fend for themselves. His face was framed by mutton-chop whiskers, according to the style of the times. He wore casual clothing but held himself with military erectness, a small belly protruding over his black leather belt, his face exuding an air of self-importance. His right arm was protectively enveloping the shoulders of a woman, considerably younger than himself, presumably his wife. She was broad-boned and wore a floral cotton dress covered with an apron of white lacy material. Rebecca looked closer at her face. She had soft yet penetrating eyes. The woman reminded Rebecca a bit of Doris Lessing – one of her grandmother's favorite authors – in an early book-jacket pose.

The other attractive, somewhat shorter woman standing beside the couple was dressed in a dark, tailored suit with her hair gathered trimly in a bun on the top of her head. Her features were dark and her general air alluring. She looked uncomfortable and out of her element.

The photograph had been taken in a high-ceilinged room in front of walls weighed down with pictures and heavy bookshelves.

Rebecca reached into the box again and dug out a pen-and-ink sketch of an Oriental man with a white headdress and wide pants and a woman in a long, black embroidered dress standing in front of a huge arched gate, with the lower reaches of one tall tower peeking out to the right and a shorter clock tower to the left. The drawing bore the following inscription: "To dear Zara, with affection, Elizabeth." It was quite well executed.

Rebecca's curiosity had been piqued.

Chapter 2

Zara Is Widowed

As Zara Rubens began to absorb the fact that her husband Daniel was gone forever, she found herself experiencing the same feelings she had felt when she and her family left Europe to come to America at the beginning of the century – grief combined with a sense of liberation. It had taken Zara time to develop a genuine attachment to Daniel but she had learned to appreciate him for his gentleness and sincerity. Yet she did not feel wholly bereft on her own.

Until Daniel's death, she never let herself imagine how life might have turned out if she had stayed behind in the shtetl and married Alex. She hadn't felt any resentment towards her family but rather an ache, a lack, similar to what she was feeling now.

She and Alex had been so alike, even though they came from different backgrounds. She was a Jewish girl from the shtetl and Alex was a rebellious youth from an Orthodox Christian family. They had met when Alex came through the Latvian villages to sell household goods to the Jews and do odd jobs. She had sat near him while he worked and laughed at his jokes, at the same time sharing with him her feelings of entrapment. Life in the shtetl was becoming unbearable for her.

One day her father caught them in a surreptitious embrace behind the back shed. This event had coincided with a series of particularly savage Cossack attacks on their village. It was decided the family would all have to leave Russia. Some of the cousins went straight on to America to be among the first Russian immigrants to that country. But Zara's family chose to try to make a place for themselves in Germany, where many Jews were doing their best to become assimilated.

Zara had been too young to accept the logic of her parents' decision. With the myopic vision of a fifteen-year-old, she had been sure she was being punished for her inappropriate behavior. She had thought of staying behind and marrying Alex, but at her age had not had the courage to believe she could survive without her family's support.

The fact that Alex was not Jewish had not been an issue for her. She remembered looking at the supposedly Jewish faces of her relatives at the time and thinking, hasn't their blood been contaminated? They can't be pure Jews. Their hair is too light, their bodies too large. But at the same time, she had been aware of her parents' deeply ingrained value system. Marrying out of the faith was equivalent to bringing about its death.

Zara thought of Cousin Rita, who had been twenty-five at the time and was now a grandmother living in Brooklyn not far from where Zara lived. Zara had once asked her why the family had left the Old Country. Rita immediately guessed what Zara was getting at. "Listen, Zarale, I hate to tell you this, but the world did not revolve around you and your needs," was her rather laconic reply, which sounded even more biting when uttered in juicy colloquial Yiddish.

The brief, excruciating efforts of Zara's family to assimilate into German society, a society even more alien than the one they had lived in for generations, finally brought them to America as well. Zara had few memories of the period in Germany since she had spent it drowning in a morass of lovelorn tears and acute culture shock. She did manage, however, to pick up German at school, which came in handy in America.

When her family arrived in New York, they discovered that many of the relatives who had preceded them had, ironically, shed their religious roots, like an old coat, casually tossing off four thousand years of history and adopting the freer ways of the American culture, which Zara's Orthodox parents had considered rather shameful.

A few months before Daniel's fatal heart attack, Zara's sister Friedl had told her that, according to a relative who had just arrived from Russia, Zara's childhood love Alex had gone off to Palestine. What could he have wanted there? Zara had no idea. He couldn't have been looking for her. He knew she had gone to Germany.

Just the mention of his name had stirred her. She tried to bring his face to mind as she had known him, but too many years had separated them for her to even remember how he had looked, let alone imagine what the years had done to his angular features. Now he was a man in his forties living Heaven knows where, probably married to some Russian woman as handsome and smart as he was.

When Friedl left she had sat transfixed for hours, unable to bring herself to get up and finish the dinner preparations. Perhaps that was why Alex came so readily to mind now that she was widowed.

Chapter 3

Conversations with Helga

Zara had one close friend in Brooklyn, with whom she had shared her most private thoughts for the past twenty-five years. Her name was Helga Ehrlich. Helga was a German immigrant and she and Zara had met when Helga had helped her make herself comprehensible to the neighborhood grocer when she first arrived. Helga had invited Zara back to her apartment for coffee and since then they had been fast friends.

Helga was short and solidly built. She wore her blond hair loosely pinned up at the back of her head, revealing a delicately carved face shielded behind unflattering, thick brown eyeglasses. She didn't care much what she wore. In the morning she would throw on the first thing that came to hand, usually some shapeless floral or striped cotton dress, which she would cover with one of her husband's oversized cardigans for warmth in winter.

She had a reserved bearing and weighed her words cautiously before opening her mouth, as if willing to stake her life on whatever came out of it. Her English was thickened by a heavy German accent but she had picked up an impressive vocabulary during her years in America and her grammar was terrifyingly impeccable.

Helga's husband, Karl, was a physician who spent long hours every day immersed in his work at Mount Sinai Hospital. Their son, Nathan, was off studying at Harvard Medical School.

The walls of their small apartment were lined with books – Karl's medical tomes, as well as the philosophy and history books that were Helga's passion. In the corner was a huge rolltop desk, the disorder of which was usually left exposed to the world. In the center of it sat a file containing Helga's latest research project. Numerous other files, articles and random pieces of semi-crumpled paper on which she had written ideas that had come to her during the day sprouted out of the various compartments of the desk as if pleading to be brought down to center stage. By the window stood an oak dining table at which Helga and Karl would have their evening meal when Karl returned from the hospital. German-language newspapers and magazines were scattered everywhere. Whenever Zara came to visit, Helga would do a quick perfunctory sweep of the room, not out of embarrassment at the disorder but for the more practical purpose of clearing enough space for them to sit and talk over coffee and cake. A small telltale cloud of dust would sometimes float up when she whisked away the papers.

Although Helga and Karl had married when Helga was still in her teens, Karl had encouraged her to continue her education. She had completed a degree at a respected German university before coming to America and had kept up her studies on her own. She wrote articles for local German magazines and when the *New York Times* opened its doors in 1851, she began writing regular pieces for them on a variety of subjects.

Zara too had a thirst for knowledge but had never had the opportunity to satisfy it. For a number of years now, Zara and Helga would meet once or twice a week. They would lounge comfortably on the Ehrlichs' overstuffed purple-and-green-striped sofa, sipping strong black coffee and eating sinful pastries from the local German bakery, while Helga helped Zara improve her English and recommended books for her to read. Zara would devour these books surreptitiously at home in the afternoons when her men were out of the house. After a while she began to frequent a Manhattan bookstore, where with the little money she was able to save by skimping on household expenses she would buy books of her own choosing. She hid the books in a suitcase until she finished them and then returned them to the store in exchange for more. She would wake up an hour or two earlier in the morning to do her chores so that she could allow herself this precious luxury.

Zara resented the couple of afternoons a week she had to spend for appearance's sake with her sisters-in-law in their spotlessly clean kitchens whose walls reeked with the odor of *shmaltz* and salted herring, and listen to the endless gossip about Uncle Anshel's inability to keep his hands to himself and Aunt Mirele's poor culinary abilities ("When they removed Feivel's gallstones everyone was sure they were really Mirele's *kneidlach*"). She could only imagine what they had to say about her on the days she didn't show up for the family dissections.

Over the years Zara had found herself becoming increasingly jealous of Daniel when he went off two evenings a week with his friends and later with their sons to study Talmud. She wished she could participate in this part of his life, although she was happy he was keeping his mind active. His work at the tailor shop would otherwise have worn him down completely.

Besides helping her with English, Helga enthusiastically imparted to Zara some of the knowledge she had acquired at university. Zara felt her mind expanding daily under the influence of Helga's tutelage. She began thinking about things she had never thought about before – politics, philosophy, history. She and Helga would sometimes argue over a point of principle, Helga becoming more and more impressed by the sharpness of Zara's mind, but Zara always acquiesced in the end even if she thought she might be right. She, of course, had never breathed a word of any of this to Daniel, although she always knew he had had his suspicions. She had found it especially difficult to conceal the enormous improvement in her English.

During their afternoon discussions Helga told Zara all about her past life in Germany, and Zara for her part would tell Helga about life in the shtetl, about the feelings of isolation and frustration she had felt and about her forbidden relationship with the Russian boy. She also described the ordeal of the short time the family had spent in Germany.

Helga came to the defense of her homeland. "I know that Germany can be a cold place, but things are changing there. We Jews are managing to win some respectability thanks to the Haskala movement. Did I ever tell you that our son is named after the main character in G.E. Lessing's play *Nathan the Wise*?"

"Who is G.E. Lessing?"

"Lessing was an eighteenth-century philosopher and writer. His play is about a wise Jewish merchant called Nathan who meets the enlightened Sultan Saladin over a chessboard in Jerusalem along with a Christian Templar. Together, they overcome the differences between Judaism, Islam and Christianity."

"It sounds fascinating but not too realistic."

"Maybe not. But we were hopeful back then. In any case, Karl and I just had no more patience for the battle, so here we are, in America, where, if you want, you can ignore religion altogether."

After Daniel died, Zara shared with her closest friend her feelings of restiveness, her desire to start a new chapter in her life, to give it the fulfillment it had not had till now. She felt she had to redefine her identity in some way.

"I've always dreamed of visiting Jerusalem," she blurted out one day after Helga had been subtly kneading at her friend's agonized ruminations. "The truth is I've never felt at home anywhere, not in Russia, certainly not in Germany and not even here in America. I remember as a child my parents toasting to 'Next year in Jerusalem' on holidays. When I was five, I decided they really meant we would be going there soon and I went to my room and packed a bag. I kept it under my bed for weeks until my mother discovered it and explained we were not really going to be leaving for Jerusalem any time in the near future.

"When I was older and read the Bible stories, I thought about what the city would look like from the drawings in the books and what it would be like to live there. I imagined myself wearing a long white dress every day and going to the well for water. My brothers, in my head, looked like brave Israelite fighters, and I saw my parents as the wise Abraham and Sarah sitting serenely at the entrance to their tent. Ridiculous, I know, but these childhood memories stick with you." Zara paused, taking a bite of fruitcake and a hearty slurp of coffee, a few drops dribbling down the bodice of her fitted blouse.

"I know my sons will think I'm out of my mind and do everything they can to stop me from going, but the truth is they don't really need me here and the more I think about going, the more determined I'm becoming."

"You do know that Jerusalem is not like the Bible stories, although the Bible stories can be pretty fierce. It's a barren, derelict place which you won't find easy to visit." Helga punctuated each significant word in the last sentence.

"I know. I've heard from people who've traveled there. But still it draws me."

Zara looked hesitantly into her friend's eyes to see how outlandish she thought her idea was. Helga remained frigidly neutral.

Zara also told Helga what Friedl had said about Alex having traveled to Palestine and how it had affected her. "I can't imagine what made him go there. We never talked about religion. We were too young to care at all about the world around us."

"Did Friedl know anything about where he is now? Is he still there?"

"I don't know. But it's not important." She brushed away the thought as quickly as she could, feeling extremely foolish.

Helga let the subject drop. After a few moments she said, "Well, if you're really serious about going, I think I might be able to help you."

"How?" Zara twisted around in her chair to get a better view of her friend.

"I knew a young British girl in Germany who now lives in Jerusalem. Her full name is Elizabeth Anne McCaul Finn. Her father, Dr. Alexander McCaul, was a well-known missionary of the London Jews' Society, a charitable organization that helps sick and poor Jews. As a child, Elizabeth traveled with her family to do missionary work in Germany, and we were neighbors.

"She is very intelligent. Without any formal education she learned to read, write and understand Hebrew, Yiddish and German. And when she arrived in Jerusalem, she also became fluent in Arabic. In one of her letters she described to me how she would ask her interpreter to teach her ten Arabic words each day, and she would write one on the fingers of each hand." Helga demonstrated by numbering off her own fingers. "Her husband became the British consul in Jerusalem about ten years ago and the two of them are deeply involved in the life there."

"Really? Tell me more." It gave Zara courage to know that a friend of Helga's was actually living there. Somehow, it made her scheme less fantastic.

"She was an amazing child and from the letters I occasionally receive from her I believe she has become a remarkable woman, someone worth traveling halfway around the world to meet."

"Do you have her address?"

"Of course. I'll go and find it. And, by the way, I suggest you get a letter of reference from the government here before you go, just in case you have some difficulties. There's not really an American consulate there, you know."

"Well, that's reassuring." Zara smirked.

"You won't be going to a fairyland, Zara. It's a place of real danger and intrigue and you've got to protect yourself."

"Now you're really scaring me," Zara answered, only half-jokingly this time.

Helga tossed her a superior stare and went off to rummage through her desk drawers for the address.

Chapter 4

Exchange of Letters between Zara and Elizabeth Finn

May 25, 1855

Dear Mrs. Finn,

I received your name and address from a dear friend of both of ours, Helga Ehrlich. She has told me a great deal about you. She remembers you as a warm, loving person and says that from your letters she guesses you have only improved over the years. I lived a couple of years in Germany as a teenager, but unfortunately, I don't remember that time very well.

I'm writing you because I've decided to visit the Holy Land this spring and Helga says you could perhaps help me find my way. I hope this is not asking too much. The truth is I don't have any real plans yet. I have recently lost my husband and have no binding responsibilities here and I thought I would come to see Jerusalem. It is a place I have dreamed to see all my life.

I know you and your husband are very busy with Mr. Finn's responsibilities as consul and your good works so I will completely understand if you do not have time for me. I would appreciate it though if you could give me some suggestions to help me prepare for the journey. If you cannot, that is fine but perhaps we will at least get a chance to meet for coffee – or perhaps tea – after I arrive.

Sincerely,

Zara Rubens

July 30, 1855

Dear Mrs. Rubens,

I was extremely pleased to receive your letter. I remember Helga fondly and do my best to keep up our correspondence.

It is true that my husband and I are kept much occupied with his consular duties and my own commitments. However, I will accept nothing less than a positive reply from you to my most heartfelt invitation to stay with us for as long as you desire.

I must prepare you, Mrs. Rubens, for the rude awakening you are about to have with regard to life in the Holy Land. Life here is in many ways the same as life anywhere, our minds usually distracted by daily worries which occupy us for the better part of the day. But these everyday occurrences take place in surroundings that have been burned in our minds from the biblical stories of our childhood. Here modern European society meets the world of the ancient Israelites, whose customs are still being practiced every day by the locals. In many ways it is a place that is only emerging from primitive barbarism. But this exciting meeting of the modern and ancient worlds produces fascinating events of great interest.

On the more practical level, I must tell you that the living standard here is in general not very high, nor is the sanitation level. As for the cultural life, it is virtually nonexistent, although we do try to provide what we can. As of late, my husband and I have begun having literary soirées at the consulate, which you might be interested in attending while you are here. My husband also gives lectures from time to time on various subjects of interest to the locals.

I hope I have not discouraged you too much as I would very much like to make your acquaintance and familiarize you with the city. In any case, I am already arranging for a room for you with the best view of the area and impatiently awaiting your arrival in the spring.

Best wishes from your new friend,
Elizabeth Anne McCaul Finn

Chapter 5

The Boat Journey to Palestine

Zara set sail on March 1, 1856. Her sons and their families were there to see her off, still reeling from her impetuous decision. Helga was there too – she had worn her one elegant suit with the fur collar in Zara's honor – and even Karl had taken off a precious hour from his work at the hospital. Zara looked at her children and grandchildren for a long moment as they all stood at the wharf chatting amongst themselves. They were the sole confirmation of what she had accomplished in her life in America. And Helga and Karl, who stood somewhat removed from the rest, were proof for her that she could now become a person in her own right.

She parted from her family with no small amount of apprehension and guilt, wondering all the time if she would ever see them again.

Then Helga came up and hugged her, the first time Zara could remember her undemonstrative friend showing any physical display of emotion. "My dear friend, I can't tell you how much I admire you. You have an honesty about you that doesn't allow for pretense on the part of anyone in your presence and a courage that will see you through whatever you may have to face. I'm so proud of you. You are going to have the experience of a lifetime. Please share it with us. Write as often as you can."

"I'll do my best. I hope the letters will get through. The mail service is not that reliable, I understand."

"Take care of yourself. And don't do anything foolish."

"I won't, don't worry. In any case, I have your friend Elizabeth to watch over me."

They found themselves embracing warmly once again, both shedding a few uncharacteristic tears. Then Zara boarded the ship.

After several days of rough seas and unpredictable spring weather, Zara finally ventured out on deck one afternoon for the first time since she had sailed. It was a cool day with a light, soothing breeze blowing from the west, but the sun shone brightly. She seemed to be the only one abroad. She settled into a deck chair to enjoy the warmth of the afternoon air.

Somewhere out of the depths of her mind emerged a memory of her journey in the opposite direction a quarter of a century earlier. It had also been spring, but much colder. She had had no conception of where she was headed then, either. The years in Germany, as much as she remembered them, had been an enormous adjustment in themselves from the life of the shtetl.

She had tried to imagine back then what New York would be like, what her life would be like. But no matter how fertile her imagination had been at the time it could in no way compete with the reality she was about to encounter, starting with the humiliations that awaited the family during their first years in the country until her father was able to establish himself in a business of his own.

She was still trying to get used to the man she had been married off to in Germany, a man she hadn't chosen, hadn't even had the chance to get to know. Fortunately for her, he had turned out to be an honest, diligent soul who was also a good father to their sons and who sincerely cared for her.

She had not expected anything more of life then. Both her parents had died from overwork a few years after their arrival in

New York. It was at that point that her rebellious spirit had been crushed. Being in a foreign country, barely knowing the language, working like a slave, having no real control over her life – all this had broken her. All she could do was throw herself into taking care of her husband and bringing up her sons as best she could.

And now she was uprooting herself again. She didn't know for how long or why.

She closed her eyes, hoping to drift off into a comforting sleep, but opened them again after a few minutes, when she felt a presence obstructing the heat of the sun. A black-suited, bearded religious Jew with scraggly earlocks, who looked much like her father had looked upon their arrival in America, had sat himself down on the deck chair beside her. This was in itself quite unusual since Ortho-dox men, Zara knew, do not usually allow themselves to fraternize with strange women. But this man seemed to be out of his element, as was she. Zara glanced at him sidewise, a bit apprehensively. She saw that he was actually quite ancient, a thin, cinereous beard barely concealing his wrinkled throat. He clearly wanted to talk.

She ventured a cautious "Good afternoon," and he responded with a heavily accented but rather cheerful "Good afternoon to you, madam." His face was sympathetic and friendly. He asked her where she was going, as the ship made a few stops along the way.

"To Palestine."

"Oh, really. I am too. For what purpose you go?"

"Just for a visit. And you?"

"Oh, I'm going there to die," he answered quite matter-of-factly. "*Ribbono shel olam*, the Master of the world, has decided that my time is coming close. I always promised to myself to be buried in Jerusalem. So it makes it much easier if I die there too. No?" He smiled sheepishly, this probably being the first time he had verbal-ized his intentions to an outsider.

Zara was taken aback by such a frank disclosure from a total stranger. She didn't quite know how to react. She knew it was the custom for Jewish elders to make the trip to Jerusalem to be buried there but she had never really talked to anyone about it. She was also struck by some of the similarities in their situations. A thousand questions rushed to her mind.

"I'm sorry to hear that you are ill. Is your family traveling with you?"

"No, I am alone. I left my wife at home with the children and the grandchildren. It is better for them there."

"It must be very difficult for you."

He didn't reply.

"May I ask you something?"

"If you like."

"Please, tell me why you are willing to leave all your loved ones and go off to die in a country you've never seen."

"You are Jewish, yes?"

"Yes."

"Then you understand when I tell you that it is a *mitzva*. It is something one must do."

"That I know. But what does your heart feel?"

"I don't usually ask myself those kinds of questions. I am a religious man. I accept what I must do."

He paused, twiddling his earlocks pensively. When he saw this answer didn't satisfy Zara's curiosity he added, "If I think about it I can tell you that I am a little frightened, as I do not know anyone over there. I have the address of a yeshiva that I can go to. I will spend the rest of my days there praying and thanking God for all the good He has done for me. People will take care of me. Jews will take care of me."

"Where do you come from originally?"

"Russia, of course."

"Wouldn't you think of going back there to die?"

"Och, no, no. Russia is a place only of poverty and suffering. I never felt I belonged there. All my life, like all good Jews, I dreamed to go home to Jerusalem and now I am going. I long to return there as a child to its mother."

This interested Zara even more. "Do you know anything about the life there?"

"I know it is not easy. It is all desert and Arabs and cruel Turks. I have heard stories. But that is not the Jerusalem I am going to. I am going to *Yerushalayim shel malla*, not *Yerushalayim shel matta*. You know what I mean?"

"Yes, I know what you mean." She had had enough of a Jewish education to understand that the old man believed he was going to what was considered the spiritual city, the one that fed the soul, not the everyday earthly city that fed the body.

"So, you understand. I must do this."

"I understand."

Zara suddenly felt very depressed. She certainly didn't identify with the old man's words. She had never been able to understand this blind faith. Or was it just plain naïveté? Was it an inherited quality? Are some people born with spirituality like black hair or brown eyes and others not? And if so, how could generations of Jews be endowed with it, then cross an ocean, remove their outer trappings and change their personalities in a generation? Was it some bizarre mental transformation for the sake of survival?

And what was she doing? What was she going to? She was not going to the Holy Land out of any faith. She had lost that a long time ago. And the way the old man described the place made Helga's and Mrs. Finn's cautionary words suddenly seem much more real.

She talked on with the old Jew for a few more minutes out of politeness and then took her leave and went back to her cabin to be alone with her thoughts. After a while, she dropped off into a merciful sleep.

When she awoke, she took out the last letter she had received from Mrs. Finn before leaving America and reread it:

December 20, 1855

Dear Zara,

I hope you don't mind me calling you Zara as I feel we are already good friends. I'm so glad that you have agreed to take us up on our offer. We are already making plans for all the places we can take you to visit and all the things we can do together. I hope we won't tire you out too much.

I just wanted to apprise you of some of the arrangements we have made for you upon your arrival. Our dragoman, Dimitri, will meet you at the Jaffa port. He'll identify you from the description you sent us. You'll ride up to Jerusalem with him in a caravan of camels and mules. The journey can be a bit arduous but Dimitri will take very good care of you. And, don't worry, even though he is Greek, he speaks a fluent English.

I envy you your first journey to Jerusalem. One's first sighting of the Holy City is a once-in-a-lifetime experience.

I hope you are bringing plenty of warm clothing. Even though this is the Middle East and it can get beastly hot, it also tends to get quite cold in the winter. It has even been known to snow!

I'm looking forward to meeting you. Have a safe journey.
Best wishes,
Elizabeth

Elizabeth's letter was so chatty, so practical and down-to-earth, so positive, that it lifted her spirits. She went off to dinner much encouraged.

Chapter 6

Zara's Journey to Jerusalem

When the ship finally docked at the Jaffa port on April 2, even before Zara set foot on land, she felt she had passed over into another world, another time. There was a lot of clamor and commotion when they disembarked, as if each and everyone there was preparing for the arrival of some important personage. The natives were dressed in a variety of ethnic costumes. Everyone was earnestly absorbed in their individual occupations, be it unloading of cargo, transporting of people and goods, or selling whatever might be in demand at whatever price could be procured.

Many of the port workers were bare-chested in the heat, and their robust, muscular bodies glistened with sweat as they heaved their loads. What struck Zara most was the colorfulness of the scene, the exotic appearance of the locals – the turbans, the long cotton shirts, the dark skin of many of them. Some of them reminded her of the Negroes she had seen working the cotton fields on a trip to the southern states a few years ago – except for the shouting, which seemed so natural to those participating in it here. To the travelers coming off the ship after a long, grueling voyage it was overpowering.

Zara had no idea how she would ever discover the dragoman that Mrs. Finn had sent to meet her but suddenly he appeared at her side.

"Good afternoon, madam."

"Good afternoon. You must be Dimitri."

"That is correct, madam. I hope your journey was not too arduous."

His use of the word "arduous" made it quite clear who was responsible for what Mrs. Finn had called this gentleman's excellent English. Zara remembered her using that exact word to describe the journey to Jerusalem in her letter.

In front of her stood a small, wiry man with a copper complexion, whose most distinguishing feature was his thick black moustaches which curled up majestically on either side of his elongated nose like decorative iron railings, reaching to the top of his earlobes. He seemed anxious to please, and after a few more short exchanges, he went off to retrieve her luggage.

As Zara stood waiting, she wondered how she appeared to him – a middle-aged American woman totally inappropriately dressed and very much out of her milieu. An article she had recently read by an American humorist came to mind. The writer had caustically recommended that his compatriots stay where they belong and not travel abroad because they always looked so horribly foolish and out of place in foreign lands. And, besides, according to the writer, the truth was they had no real chance of comprehending the countries they were visiting in the short time they had allowed themselves to do so. Perhaps he was right, she thought.

Before she knew what was happening Dimitri had returned with her luggage and was loading it onto two camels. This was her first encounter with a camel. She found it to be a rather peculiar creature and quite intimidating in size.

Fortunately, she soon learned she would be riding not on a camel but on a horse, which, considering the length of the journey, was not an experience she anticipated with much joy either. Dimitri helped her mount. She was surprised to discover that its Arabian saddle was actually quite comfortable. It was provided, both back and front, with an elevated support, and the stirrups, which were as large as a pair of shoe soles, were very convenient as braces for her feet.

As they set out, she noticed that the aged Orthodox Jew she had conversed with on the ship was joining their caravan as well. This, on one hand, somewhat reassured her since she at least was acquainted – however briefly – with someone in the group, but on the other hand, his presence brought back the feelings of melancholy their conversation had awakened in her.

While they negotiated the dreary desert path, Dimitri acted as her guide, even though there wasn't much to describe. On the way, all she could make out was stony, dry land with hardly a tree or shrub to relieve the monotony. Only a few olive trees, some prickly pears, thistle and tumbleweed seemed to have remained loyal to this infertile soil. The milk and honey of the land of the chosen people had not been flowing for quite a long time, if it had ever done so. The sun beat down mercilessly on their heads. Swarms of gnats pestered them constantly. Zara soon found it necessary to reinforce her flimsy straw hat, which was continually threatening to fly off into the endless infinity of the desert, with a long, white silk scarf – one that she normally reserved for more elegant occasions.

Zara saw the old man being jolted along in front of her, shakily holding a large checkered handkerchief over his mouth to shield him from the sand that billowed up around them. Every mile seemed to cause him more and more discomfort. She wondered what his feelings now were about returning to the bosom of his homeland. Not that she was any more pleased about her decision at this juncture herself.

When they stopped to rest, Dimitri began to acquaint her with some of the local customs. He cooked up some thick black coffee over a small fire he had quickly put together and offered her a sweetmeat called baklava, a layered dessert made with paper-thin sheets of dough and filled with chopped nuts, "all of which are soaked in honey and rosewater," he explained. Zara thought of bringing bring back some to her friends and family – if and when she ever returned.

Dimitri had a reassuring manner about him. Despite the rather disconcerting pistol and saber emerging like two exclamation points from either side of his wide trousers, he seemed a gentle, almost poetic, soul who had received some education in the finer arts of living.

Searching for a topic of conversation, she asked him why it was necessary for them to travel in a caravan.

"Well, you see, madam, although you have nothing to worry about – let me emphasize that, please – there are some around here who might sometimes steal from people traveling through the desert like this. We will, for instance, be passing by a village called Abu Ghosh, whose people have been known to rob pilgrims traveling up to Jerusalem, despite the fact that they are paid a generous *baksheesh* every year to prevent them from doing such things."

Even though Zara was not yet familiar with the word *baksheesh*, it was easy enough to determine that it was some kind of bribe offered these natives to keep them from interfering with passing travelers. Zara would soon learn to what extent this custom was an integral part of the local way of life.

The redoubtable sheik of this Arab town, according to Dimitri, had once even had the audacity to murder two Turkish pashas passing through the area – "but that was several years ago," he added with a halfheartedly reassuring smile.

After the small break for refreshments, they all began to re-mount their horses. Suddenly, there was a flurry around the old Jew, who seemed to be unable to get up. As she moved closer, Zara saw he had been accidentally trampled by his horse while trying to mount it. Dimitri immediately took charge. He explained to her that he was going off to get some help and would be back presently. There was nothing to worry about, he explained, as there were several people around to protect her if they were attacked. In any case, he would warn the people in Abu Ghosh that such a rash act would be highly inadvisable. He claimed that his word would carry a great deal of weight coming from a servant of the British consul. And off he galloped.

Zara did not particularly find his reassurances calming but she had no choice but to accept the situation. She approached the old Jew to see if there was anything she could do to help. It took all his strength for him to shake his aged head in the negative. She tried to make him as comfortable as possible. Suddenly, he grabbed her arm roughly and drew her down towards him.

"Please promise you will see I am buried on the Mount of Olives," he whispered into her ear. "I have come all this way. Please do that for me."

Zara was quite taken aback, since she had no idea what his request demanded of her, but she replied that she would do her best to fulfill his wishes. "And in any case," she said, "I'm sure you will come out of this all right. It's doubtlessly just a minor injury."

She had no sooner finished her sentence when the man fell back in a swoon, hit his head on the rock it had been resting on, and died. There was a moment of ethereal silence among the members of the convoy. When they recovered, the Christians among them crossed themselves; the Moslems uttered a hushed prayer, while the Jews recited the *Shema*. Zara was too dazed to do a thing. Someone respectfully covered the old man with a camel blanket and they all waited for Dimitri's return.

Dimitri came back soon after with a local doctor. Zara drew her guide aside and explained what had transpired between the old man and herself before his death. Dimitri was perturbed but did what had to be done without a second's hesitation. He called over one of the camel drivers, slipped him a fistful of coins, and sent him off to Jerusalem to bring back a rabbi who would take care of things.

While they waited once more, this time for the return of the camel driver and the rabbi, Zara thirstily finished off the last bit of water she had left in her leather drinking pouch and went to seek some solitude on a nearby hill to mull over the tangle of thoughts and emotions churning up inside her.

This encounter had suddenly brought home to her the awareness that she had entered a world as precarious as the one her parents had left a quarter of a century earlier. Here, too, long life could not be guaranteed by how pious you were or by how many bribes you were willing to pay. The spiritual city that the old man had been making his way towards was certainly a chimeric dream world where reason and logic would not guarantee survival. The alternative seemed to be adopting a submissive attitude which might help one stoically accept whatever life held in store. And life in this God-forsaken country, she feared, was full of unexpected and unwelcome surprises. She envisioned herself shedding the veneer of order and respectability her family had worked so hard to acquire in America and recreating herself in some other image, the nature of which was yet unclear to her.

When the camel driver finally returned with the rabbi, the members of the caravan were all resting quietly under the few trees that provided minimal protection from the relentless afternoon sun. The camel driver forced his animal to kneel down, and he and a few others carefully loaded the body of the old Russian wrapped in the camel blanket onto its back. They draped him over the two sides of the beast like a rolled rug. The camel then rose gracefully on command, in bestial obliviousness to the poignancy of the moment, and was slowly led off. Thus this tiny caravan rode back to Jerusalem with the camel driver at its head, followed by the camel laden with the lifeless body of the old Jew, and the rabbi on a horse. Before leaving, the rabbi assured Zara that the old man would receive the proper burial he had requested.

The rest of the caravan then remounted their horses, each with the attentive assistance this time of a dragoman to avoid any further mishaps, and headed off to Jerusalem as well.

Chapter 7

Zara's Arrival in Jerusalem

Late in the day, after riding past a few picturesque, misleadingly peaceful Arab villages bordered by olive groves and cornfields, the caravan arrived at the outer reaches of Jerusalem. Rain clouds hung over the city, like the forces of some enemy power poised to swoop down on the town. In the crepuscular silence, Zara's initial impression was of a small, unimposing fortress. It took all her childhood memories of the tales of Abraham, King David and King Solomon to accord to what her eyes beheld the historical significance she felt it surely warranted. The strong emotions that Mrs. Finn promised would be hers did not well up in her throat. Perhaps the events leading up to her arrival had outrivaled them in immediacy. Or perhaps this was a city that inspired awe and dignity, which do not find appropriate expression in tearful exuberance.

Dimitri hurried them along so they would reach Jaffa Gate before the Turkish sentinel barred it for the night. He explained that the doors are locked from the second hour after sunset until the break of dawn and that armed guards stand at the gates night and day.

"At noon on Friday, all the gates are closed," he continued, "because Friday is the Moslem day of rest and they all go to the hour of prayer on the Temple Mount. Even the pasha and his soldiers go.

33

That is why they close the gates. Fools believe this is to prevent the Messiah of Israel from entering Jerusalem; they claim the Jewish Messiah will enter Jerusalem on a Friday at noon. Mrs. Finn has explained to me that this cannot be possible since the Bible says the son of David will not arrive on a Sabbath eve. In any case, the gates are reopened two hours later."

As they stopped at their last resting place before entering the city the Christian and Moslem pilgrims ceremoniously sank to their knees and thanked their respective deities for the honor that had been bestowed upon them of entering into the Holy City in their lifetime. The Jews swayed back and forth in silent prayer. A few shed a tear or two. Zara could not help but think of the poor old Jew who had been denied this experience.

Once they had passed through the gate successfully, Dimitri soon brought her to the door of the British Consulate, just beyond Jaffa Gate, and bid her farewell. She thanked him for his devoted care and tried to bestow upon him what she thought was a generous recompense for his not-insignificant efforts on her behalf. He rejected her offer with a brush of his sinewy hand, saying he had already been amply compensated by the consul's wife.

And then, before she could feel a moment of loss or loneliness or fear, a gentle, loving hand was placed on her shoulder and she turned to face the woman whom she sensed instantly would have a profound effect on this next chapter in her life – Elizabeth Anne McCaul Finn. They embraced as if they were already old friends and, without delay, Mrs. Finn guided Zara into the living quarters of the consulate building.

"My husband, James," she explained, "is presently taken up with consular duties, but he has promised to give us his full attention after nine o'clock, at which time we will dine together and hear all about your adventures. In the meantime perhaps you would like a cup of tea to get the dirt of the road out of your throat before you go to your quarters to rest."

Zara immediately gave herself up to this woman's charge. She was led directly into the sitting room of the consulate quarters. While Elizabeth Finn was looking to the tea, Zara picked up an impressive volume on the table beside her entitled *Walks about Jerusalem* by W. H. Bartlett. After leafing through it for a minute or two her eye was drawn to several romantic paintings of the surrounding area that were hanging on the walls. Among them was a painting of a rather melancholy-looking, mustachioed Englishman dressed in Turkish garb. He looked as if he would have little skill in the use of the menacing saber hanging at his side. The painting was entitled "David Roberts Esq. in the Dress He Wore in Palestine."

On her return with the tea tray, Mrs. Finn observed Zara's interest in the paintings. "Those are copies of paintings done about fifteen years ago by a British painter called David Roberts on his visit to the Holy Land." She then proceeded to tell Zara his life story in meticulous detail.

"Roberts," she said, "was of Scottish descent. He started as an apprentice to a house painter and went on to paint scenery for a traveling circus and later for Covent Garden Opera. But what he really wanted to be was a landscape painter. He worked hard at it and gradually acquired a number of important patrons. He then put his mind to learning how to do quick sketches in preparation for the trip he decided to make to Egypt and Palestine.

"His goal was to draw the famous ruins and biblical locations. Since few people journey much beyond their hometowns, travel being so difficult and expensive, printed books of landscape and travel drawings are for most people their only window to the outside world. They have become quite a popular form of entertainment, and people are willing to spend great sums to collect either journals that include small sketches of holy places or full-blown art books, especially of the Near East. So he hoped there would be a great market in England and Europe for images of such exotic subjects.

"In any case, Roberts was a man endowed with a very romantic spirit and he was willing to take the financial risk. He arrived here in the spring of 1839 – despite warnings that the city was infested with the plague – dressed in Turkish garb to disguise himself and protect him and his companions from marauding bandits."

"I take it that is what that painting commemorates," said Zara, pointing to the portrait on the wall.

"That's right, and the other paintings are copies of some of his most famous depictions of Jerusalem." She pointed out each in turn. "This is the Mosque of Omar from Mount Moriah, this a view of the Tower of David, the one on the far wall is of the Damascus Gate, and next to it is a drawing of Bethlehem from afar. The one behind you is of the famous Church of the Nativity inside the town of Bethlehem itself. His lack of any political interests made him a very judicious chronicler of these sights, I believe.

"As for the book you're holding, that is a rather scholarly volume written and illustrated by another British traveler, which gives a very detailed account of his visit to Jerusalem in 1842. Unfortunately, on the way back from his third visit to the country a couple of years back, Bartlett met his death by drowning somewhere between Malta and Marseille. You're welcome to borrow the book if you wish."

"I'd like that. Thank you."

"But you'll have plenty of time later to hear and see everything. Now tell me a little about your journey here." Mrs. Finn directed Zara to a comfortable armchair, while she pulled up a straight-backed, slatted wooden one for herself. She sat erect, her unadorned hands clasped in eager virtuousness.

Zara proceeded to tell her in some detail about the voyage over, of her conversation with the aged Russian Jew, and about his later sad demise.

Mrs. Finn suddenly froze. "What's wrong?" Zara asked. "Have I offended you in some way?"

"No, not at all. It's just that I had a similar experience on my first journey up to Jerusalem. My father was also attempting to fulfill a lifelong wish to visit the Holy City before he died, and he also expired on his way up to the city. It sounds like it happened at almost the exact same spot where your old Jew died and under virtually identical circumstances. I spent my first months here recovering from the shock with the help of some very dear English friends, the Andersens, and of my dear brother Walter, who arrived a while after I did."

"What a dreadful coincidence," was all Zara could think to say.

Mrs. Finn paused for a long moment. "I wonder how much of a coincidence it really is. We Christians and Jews are not so very different. This old Jew and my father both had this longing to touch the soil of Jerusalem before they died. They both unfortunately waited a little too long to fulfill their wish."

"That was one of the things the old man" – Zara suddenly realized she hadn't even learned his name – "and I talked about. Perhaps you can explain to me, Mrs. Finn –"

"Elizabeth, please."

"Elizabeth," Zara repeated dutifully. "I understand that you and your husband have a strong connection to the Jews living here. Please tell me, why do Jews only come to the Holy Land to die?"

"Ah, now that is a very good question. In my opinion, they don't come sooner mainly because the thought of living here has never been a tangible reality for them. And perhaps it's understandable – life here is no bed of roses, as I tried to explain to you in my letters. My husband will most likely elaborate on the subject this evening."

"But tell me then, do you think they will ever believe otherwise?" Zara persisted. "What might bring them to believe that they can actually live their lives here?"

"Only God knows that." Elizabeth paused again for a few long seconds. And then she asked, "But tell me, Zara, why have *you* come here?"

It was Zara's turn to pause, as she had no ready answer to that question. She took a long sip of tea before speaking.

"I don't really know. It seemed the right thing to do at this point in my life. My family and friends thought I was out of my mind, perhaps going through some crisis after losing my husband not long ago. And maybe that's true. But I think it's more than that. I think I've come to satisfy some need in my life. Not religious, I don't think, but something spiritual that I can't really define."

"The distance between what we call formal religion and our personal spiritual feelings is not really that great, you know. But let me tell you at the outset that, although my husband and I do our best to help Jews see the light of Christianity, we have had some unpleasant experiences in which several of our converts have suffered considerable pain during and after their conversion process and we have learned to be very cautious in our missionary work since then."

Zara was very relieved to hear this. Elizabeth then suggested she go settle in and return for dinner. Zara was glad to finally have some time to herself.

Chapter 8

Dinner with the Finns

The consulate was attached to the Protestant Christ Church. Actually, the British had received permission to build the church by claiming it was meant to be the chapel of the consulate. This was supposed to be a temporary solution until the actual British Consulate was constructed. As living quarters for a family of five it was quite unsuitable. The two main sitting rooms had been combined into one larger one by the Finns to provide the consul adequate space to carry out his business and receive visitors. The family had the use of only one small sitting room of their own. There was no place for the servants to live on the premises and certainly no room for guests.

In short, it was impossible for Zara to stay in the consulate building so Elizabeth had found her a place nearby – rather spartan quarters, but they were clean and adequate for her needs. And as promised, they provided a charming view of the Hinnon Valley below Mount Zion and a peek at the hills leading down to Jericho. It was necessary for the consul's janissary, or *kawwas*, to escort Zara to and from her lodgings since no one was allowed to be abroad at night due to the danger of thieves. Only Jews on their way to synagogue to recite midnight prayers were permitted to walk outside within their quarter.

At exactly nine o'clock Zara was brought back to the consulate by the dutiful *kawwas*. The heavy clouds, which had earlier threatened rain, were releasing their weighty load and, despite the short distance she had to cover, Zara was wet through by the time she arrived at the Finns. Elizabeth fussed over her with a towel until she was sufficiently satisfied that Zara was dry enough to keep at bay any attack of influenza. There was a large fire blazing in the living room at which Elizabeth insisted Zara have the central position.

Once all this was settled Zara was then introduced to the consul. James Finn was not a very tall or imposing man but he gave the impression of great determination behind his modest exterior. Zara found his steadfast gaze somewhat disconcerting but once he began speaking she quickly got over her uneasiness.

"Welcome, Mrs. Rubens. We are so glad to have you with us. I am terribly sorry we could not accommodate you in the parsonage itself. The allowances allotted to us are far from adequate, I'm afraid. So you will have to forgive us our meager offerings. Fortunately, my dear wife knows how to make a very little go a long way."

Before they sat down to dinner, Elizabeth insisted the three of them pose for a photographic portrait. Apparently, photography was one of her passions. While Elizabeth was setting up the camera and preparing it for the photograph James extolled his wife's many talents to Zara.

"You'll have to excuse her, but she is quite obsessed with photography. In fact, she is a pioneer in the art. She also does her best to support local photographers. But this, by the way, is only one of her talents. She is also a prodigious pen-and-ink sketch artist. She has done some remarkable drawings of Biblical and historical landscapes. If you give her the slightest encouragement, she'll be glad to show you a few."

By this time Elizabeth was satisfied that everything for the photograph was ready. She emerged from under the black cloth and directed two servants to handle the flash tray and take the actual picture. When she was satisfied they were clear about their tasks, she took her place between her husband and Zara and instructed them to proceed.

There was a sudden ear-shattering bang and all three of them found themselves totally blinded by the light of the flash. Elizabeth apologized for the inconvenience but promised them the photograph would be worth the discomfort.

They then found their way as best they could to the dinner table, still somewhat discombobulated by the experience. It was only the three of them, as the Finns' three children had been sent off to bed an hour or so earlier. They were served an adequate, although rather bland, evening meal.

After Zara brought the consul up to date on her eventful arrival, she returned to her preoccupation with the custom of Jews coming to the Holy Land solely to spend their final days.

"The lot of the Jews here is certainly not an easy one," he responded. He then proceeded to launch into a lengthy explanation of the status of the British Consulate in Jerusalem and its treatment of the Jews who had come under its protection. This was clearly a speech he had given several times before. As he spoke, he occasionally glanced over to his wife for reassurance.

"Until the British Consulate was established in 1838 – actually the first consulate in the country – there was no rule of law in the land besides the corrupt, self-serving administration of the Moslems. For this reason generations of European Jews were too fearful to come and live in Palestine. In 1839, Lord Palmerston, the British foreign secretary, directed his first consul in Jerusalem to provide protection to the Jews generally, thus giving them recognition as a nation unto themselves. In 1840, however, the Jews in Damascus suffered severe persecution as a result of a blood libel against them. They were falsely accused of drinking the blood of a Capuchin friar named Thomas during their Passover holiday. In 1841, when the Turks returned to power after a nine-year interlude of more liberal Egyptian rule, the British consul was ordered to make known to the local authorities that the British government felt responsible for the welfare of the Jews and were concerned they be protected from discrimination.

"When I first became consul in 1846 there were several incidents concerning persecution of Jews that I did my best to correct. In one case at least, I know my intervention did sway the pasha's handling of the incident.

"I was one day approached by a group of very anxious Jews. Their chief rabbi had been accused of murdering a Moslem muleteer and the Jewish dragoman had been arrested until the matter could be resolved. The Jews explained that a man by the name of Solomon Aglai had been traveling one night to Jaffa and he and his Moslem muleteer had been set upon and robbed and the muleteer murdered. According to them, some malevolent individual had informed the pasha that the chief rabbi of the Jews had ordered the murder. I immediately looked into the matter and satisfied myself that these accusations had no basis in fact. I knew I had to act quickly as I was extremely concerned about the greater repercussions of such an affair for the Jewish community as a whole. After consulting with my superiors in England I took steps to have the charges dropped and the case was immediately closed."

Zara could see that the consul was quite pleased with himself for having managed to bring the affair to a satisfactory conclusion.

He continued. "There was another incident, in which a Jew of Russian origin, who had just arrived to the country and was ignorant of local customs, was attacked and almost killed by a crowd of Christian extremists for crossing the square in front of the Church of the Holy Sepulcher. Since the poor man received no aid from his own consul, I intervened with the pasha and obtained the release of the Jew. As a result of that incident the Foreign Office issued an instruction that the English consul should defend any European Jew from persecution, be he Russian, Austrian or French, if he was unable to receive protection from his own consul."

He looked up at his guest again to see the effect of his monologue upon her. Zara gave him a polite smile but did not respond.

"But I digress. As for your question, Mrs. Rubens, I must tell you that there *are* Jews who look on this country as a future home for their people and not just as a last stop on the way to the graveyard. There is one important event in that regard which I would like to share with you, a visit to Jerusalem of the remarkable philanthropist Sir Moses Montefiore.

"Sir Moses and his elegant wife arrived last summer accompanied by Colonel Gawler, an especially colorful figure, decked out in a flamboyant white-plumed hat and a bemedaled scarlet uniform. The local Jews came out in full force to greet him, led by the chief rabbi and his deputies. They, as well as Jerusalemites of other ethnic groups, swarmed the path he was to follow into the city. This was quite an unusual occurrence since Jews rarely leave the city unless to occasionally visit their holy places in Bethlehem and Hebron. In fact, they are generally quite wary of going out en masse in public at any time.

"Sir Moses and his entourage greeted the crowd before entering the city and then proceeded directly to the synagogue. After his visit there it was my great honor to introduce him to the pasha and from there I took him to view the site of the Second Temple from the roof of the army barracks. I could see he was deeply moved by what his eyes beheld. He then took his leave of us with promises to soon return and went on to visit Hebron, before taking a boat home from Jaffa."

Montefiore, a wealthy Jewish stockbroker from London, Zara learned, initiated a few projects on behalf of the Jews at the time. Two of them were the introduction of a printing press and a textile factory. He also began planning the establishment of several Jewish agricultural settlements in the country. During his visit his people handed out a silver dollar to every Jewish man, woman and child in the city. Finn explained that this was his way of taking an accurate census of the Jewish population. Montefiore was well aware the rabbis would not allow the people to be counted, a Jewish prohibition since the disastrous effects of King David's census so many centuries ago.

"The most significant benefit of this monumental visit," Finn continued, "is that it has given many Jews in Palestine new hope. Despite the persecution they continue to endure here, they now feel that somewhere in Europe there is an influential figure representing their interests.

"In my opinion," concluded Finn, "Montefiore's efforts to bring the Jews to a reasonable level of self-sufficiency is his greatest achievement. It means they will no longer have to rely so heavily on the mercy of their brethren abroad. This seems to me a much healthier approach to their situation."

After this rather lengthy address the consul excused himself, saying he had to return to his duties but that he hoped the three of them would spend the next day together viewing some of the city. Zara thanked him for his hospitality and he left.

"He'll work now for hours," explained Elizabeth. "After that he'll spend time studying subjects that interest him. He's learning Hebrew these days on his own and seems to be progressing rapidly. You should know, Zara, that my husband is highly respected here as a man of his word and as a person one can look to in time of need. He is willing to endanger himself if necessary, doing his duty without fear, even venturing out alone at night if he thinks justice can be served."

Elizabeth Finn herself seemed no less remarkable to Zara. Although Zara knew she was in a country not lacking in what Mrs. Finn had called "primitive barbarians," there were also, Zara guessed, more than a few individuals of outstanding character. She looked forward to meeting more of them.

Chapter 9

A Visit to the Wall

When Zara woke the next morning she discovered that every bone and muscle in her body had a complaint of its own to air. Despite the relatively comfortable Arabian saddle, the journey up to Jerusalem had taken its toll. She considered herself to be in good physical condition but the vagaries of the previous day had made her feel a good twenty years beyond her age.

She dragged herself out of bed at seven, as she knew the *kawwas* would be knocking on the door promptly at eight. And so he did. In his dour, officious manner, without exchanging a word with her, he led her back again to the Finns where a typical English breakfast awaited her; the only departure from her usual breakfast fare was the serving of pita bread instead of the dark loaves she was accustomed to at home.

"I hope you have slept well, Mrs. Rubens," said the consul.

"I have, thank you, sir. The room is quite pleasant." Zara directed the last remark more to Mrs. Finn than to her husband, knowing she had been responsible for procuring it.

The consul sat stiffly at the head of the table enjoying the banter of his young children, who were imparting the events of the previous day in a very adult fashion. Little five-year-old Constance contributed an elaborate tale of an encounter with an Arab boy in the street. Zara could see James's mind was soon preoccupied with the worries of his office, while Elizabeth hovered around seeing to everyone's needs and helping their two-year-old son finish up his food.

Although James was already fifty and Elizabeth more than ten years younger than Zara, the Finns gave the impression of being compatible, each taking on their role in raising a family and fulfilling their duties with dignity and grace. Zara began to reflect on her life with Daniel at this stage in their marriage. They had had some very good years together while bringing up the boys. And even some passionate moments as well, she remembered, blushing at the inappropriateness of these memories suddenly flooding her mind.

When breakfast was over the table was quickly cleared so the room could serve as a reception area once again for the consul's daily meetings with the locals. But since James had promised to dedicate the day to Zara he gave his staff a few instructions and let them go. He then invited her to accompany him and his wife to the morning prayers at the Christ Church, to which the parsonage was attached. There was a large courtyard in front, bathed in the bright morning sun and spotlessly clean. The other buildings across the courtyard, she was told, were occupied by German and English clerics and officials.

The parsonage and the church were built from the same heavy, local Jerusalem stone, giving them the air of permanence and respectability that seemed to faithfully reflect their status, although as Zara later learned permanence here was actually a relative thing. The craggy surface of the Jerusalem stone could be somewhat menacing when shrouded in the ethereal play of shade and light at certain times of the day.

The décor of the interior of the church was in the English style, modest but tasteful. The ceiling and benches were covered in dark wooden paneling. The church, as Zara was told, was also known as "the Jewish Church," being deliberately built to resemble a synagogue. Most of the lettering used in it was in Hebrew, and most of the symbolism Jewish.

The atmosphere that morning was subdued. Zara took time to look around during the service. She had never attended an Anglican church before and felt quite out of place. It all seemed incongruous with the life outside the complex, although what more appropriate locale could there be for Christians to pray in than the city where Christ had spent much of his life and where he had died? There were about a dozen worshippers that morning scattered around the pews, each absorbed in his or her own personal dialogue with God. James explained that most of the participants were foreigners, mainly British. Some of them were residents of Jerusalem, others travelers, glad to avail themselves of the opportunity to attend a Christian service in the Holy Land. There were also a number of Jewish converts.

"Prayers are held here in English in the morning, in German in the afternoon and on Sunday there are prayers in Arabic for the local converts," the consul explained in a whisper.

Once the service was over, they headed towards the Western Wall, which James believed it was his duty to show his Jewish visitor. The city was filled to overflowing because of the approaching holidays. There was a powerful feeling of anticipation in the air. Zara was told the city doubled in population during the annual pilgrimage festivals.

Zara and the Finns were escorted by the ever-present *kawwas*, in full regalia today, as he wasn't just leading Zara but the consul and his wife. He preceded them carrying a silver-headed staff of office, ceremoniously clearing the path ahead. As they walked, the local people stood up to salute the consul. Zara felt quite uneasy with this attention, unlike the consul who seemed to bask in it.

As they proceeded, James told Zara a bit about his *kawwas*. "He was a captain of the Camel Commissariat to Ibrahim Pasha's army during the interlude of Egyptian rule about twenty years ago.

He has often demonstrated his loyalty and courage in some very difficult situations."

The road they were walking along followed a direct course to the Wall reminiscent of the main thoroughfare during the time of the Romans. It was ten to fifteen feet wide and unevenly paved. A narrow canal almost two feet deep ran down its center, along which flowed the detritus of the pack animals, as well as rubbish the locals let fall. It exuded a dreadful odor. Zara wondered to herself what it would be like in the summer heat.

But as inadequate as this road was, it was broader than the narrow, meandering lanes that branched off to the right and left of it. "Many are cul-de-sacs," explained James, "leading to groups of houses or to ruins and deserted areas."

Their entourage did its best to make its way along the upper levels of the main road on either side of the sunken channel but, despite the efforts of the *kawwas*, they were often waylaid. The faithful servant had to demonstrate his not-insignificant authority, for example, in the face of a scrawny youth pushing up the road a green, blue and red wooden cart almost twice his size filled with his treasure of fruits and vegetables. The boy was quite upset at losing his hard-earned momentum. A more difficult adversary was an animal driver who demanded the right of way for himself and his emaciated pack animal where there was only enough room for two people or an animal to pass at a time. But the *kawwas* had to be most aggressive with a couple of Turkish officers who considered their status superior to that of any British intruders.

"An Arab who has a thousand words to express a camel, a sword, a mare, has scarcely one word which suggests a street," observed Elizabeth amusedly as they waited for this particular negotiation to be completed.

Despite the disruption, James returned to the subject of the Jews and his impressions of them during his service in the country. Zara knew this was all for her benefit but she felt a bit uncomfortable being singled out as a representative of her race. She did not really consider herself qualified to be one, and besides, these people were not what she considered brethren.

"There are Jews who are disrespectful and unappreciative, like many people of other religions, but despite their obvious faults, which usually manifest themselves solely within their own community, they do not attempt to have an undue influence on the society in which they live. In fact, they are almost slavishly acquiescent to the demands of their rulers.

"On a personal note I must say that many of them have shown great kindness to my wife and me during difficult periods in our lives, including praying for us at the Western Wall at the time of our child's illness and death. I have often said that these people are for me the closest in nature to the English in their moral and familial behavior."

Zara felt he was making a supreme effort to be sympathetic to the Jews for her benefit but his feelings of superiority did not escape her.

They finally arrived at the Western Wall of the Temple Mount, also known as the Wailing Wall. After all Zara had heard about it during her childhood, and all the expectations and hopes that surrounded it, she was shocked to see an unimpressive, desolate fragment of a wall which James said was no more than thirty or so yards long. "The Wall above ground," he explained, "consists of twenty-four rows of stones from different periods."

Gray stone hovels inhabited by poor Moslem families came within ten feet of the Wall itself. In between ran a dank, narrow alley scarcely one hundred feet in length and ten feet wide. Its ends were blocked by other structures. The closeness of the area seemed a breeding ground for confrontation.

James proceeded to tell Zara the history of the Wall since Second Temple times, most of which she was familiar with, but she listened politely and even learned a thing or two.

"Since the size of the Jewish population in the Land of Israel has begun to grow from the beginning of this century, and since many more visitors have come, the popularity of the Western Wall has grown considerably." James thus concluded his lecture.

There were only a few unkempt supplicants at the Wall when they arrived, praying fervently. Zara was struck by the contrast between the emotional intensity of their prayers and the reserved Anglican prayer she had witnessed earlier.

"By the afternoon," Elizabeth said, "this small area will be overcrowded with Jews, some dressed like eighteenth-century Polish noblemen – apparel totally unsuited to the oppressive heat of Jerusalem. They wear black coats or white or striped silk caftans, belted at the waist like dressing gowns, black or white leggings and, on holidays, some even wear regal fur hats."

This was a sight Zara had been familiar with in her youth and later in the religious Jewish areas of New York City. But she hadn't known that these distinctive ultra-Orthodox costumes were worn here because of a seventeenth-century Ottoman law in Jerusalem. Each nation, she was told, was required to wear its own costume so as to clearly distinguish between them. Zara wondered, then, why this anachronistic apparel had endured in the West as well.

According to James, Jews had to pay a large *baksheesh* each year to the effendi whose house adjoined the Wall for permission to pray there. There were always complaints of continued harassment by Moslems – human excrement thrown at rabbis on their way to the Wall, stones dropped from a nearby roof, sheep driven repeatedly past the Wall during morning prayers.

"When Sir Moses Montefiore saw the conditions under which the Jews were forced to pray at the Wall, he tried in vain to obtain permission to place benches or provide protection against rain. But he did manage at least to get the powers that be to pave the street. From time to time a table for the reading of the Torah is placed near the Wall, but is soon removed at the demand of the Waqf, the Moslem religious authorities." James was clearly frustrated at having to deal with such small-minded rulers.

The Finns allowed Zara some privacy to approach the Wall. She covered her head with the black shawl she had brought and walked forward. She stood there for a few minutes praying briefly, more out of duty than piety. From the corner of her eye, she could see a few men on the other side of the religious divide furtively examining her.

So this is what is left of the spiritual center of the Jewish people, she thought. This is what has stirred Jews through the centuries, a few meters of stone wall, dotted with brambles, and small notes left by hopeful supplicants. But despite herself, facing the immensity of the stones at such close proximity made the Wall seem quite formidable. She was more moved than she had expected to be. This was somehow for her the moment when she felt she had fulfilled the family promise of "Next year in Jerusalem." Beyond that, though, she couldn't imagine what further significance the experience could hold for her.

She returned to the Finns, letting her shawl slip slowly back to her shoulders as she walked. She smiled at them uneasily as they scrutinized her face to see the effect of the experience upon her. They didn't ask her anything, nor did she volunteer an expression of her feelings.

After a moment or two, James extended his right arm with a majestic flourish in the direction of the street and they silently took their leave.

On the way back they passed through the produce market, resplendent with stalls of ruby-red strawberries, scarlet tomatoes, cucumbers and luxurious purple eggplants, as well as other vegetables Zara could not identify – all grown, she was told, in areas outside Jerusalem. Many Arab girls in gay clothing were seated near their baskets of garden produce, their eyes bright, their bangles shining. They would stretch out an eager hand with a tomato or cucumber for the entourage to examine. James's *kawwas* would not prevent them from approaching but kept close watch to make sure the gestures remained innocent.

Elizabeth stopped to purchase a few vegetables, skillfully examining each one before choosing, as if she planned to serve them for tomorrow's breakfast to no less a personage than the pasha himself.

Arab men in rough, homespun garments stood about with staffs in their hands. There was something imperious in their bearing. They seemed to live a life superior to this city life, as if they had come to Jerusalem from some far-off desert village with green date palms overtopping immaculate white homes. They stared at these foreigners with cold attention, as hawks scrutinize pigeons. They were the sentinels of Arab tradition keeping a close watch on any intruders that might interfere with it, a role they had played often over the centuries. Zara passed close to one of them. A curious odor emanated from him. It was like a mixture of stale milk and the smoke of a campfire.

Zara refused Elizabeth's offer to come for tea at the end of their excursion. She wanted to return to her room and absorb the myriad of impressions she had experienced during the day.

Chapter 10

A Letter to Helga

April 1856

Dearest Helga,

I hope this letter won't take too long to reach you as I am sending it off with some acquaintances of the Finns who are sailing for America tomorrow.

I trust all is well with you and that you are enjoying your rich and active life, as only you know how to do. I miss you sorely.

First of all, I want to thank you for introducing me to the Finns. They have been tremendously generous with their time and affection. I have learned so much from them already that I feel I don't know where to put all this knowledge and emotion.

I want to share with you an experience I had yesterday at the Church of the Holy Sepulcher that will give you a clue of what my life has been like here since I arrived. Please don't show this letter to the boys, as I don't want them to worry about me.

While you are reading, I would like you to consider an idea that has been brewing in my mind over the last few days. Life is so dramatic and so different than anyone in America could imagine that I thought I might write down some of my experiences and offer them to the New York Times as a foreign travel correspondent. I think it will both help me digest what I am going through and serve as a possible source of income for me. Beyond that, it will be a way for me to share everything with my friends and family at home. I am turning to you to make the offer to the paper if you think the idea is worthy, as

I know you have good connections with some of the editors there.

My main concerns are these: Is this something I want my family to read about? Perhaps I should write the articles under a pen name. And, of course, I wonder if these stories will be of interest to anyone over there. Please let me know what you think. I'll continue to write down my impressions until I get a response from you.

Yours always,
Zara

THE HOLY FIRE CEREMONY

I was fortunate to be invited by Elizabeth Finn, the wife of the British consul in Jerusalem, to participate in a most unusual Orthodox Christian ritual known as the Ceremony of the Holy Fire, an event that serves as the climax of their Easter celebrations. It takes place on Holy Saturday at the Church of the Holy Sepulcher, in the presence of the Greek Orthodox and Armenian patriarchs.

The consul, James Finn, explained to me that there were numerous travelers this year from America, as well as from the various countries of Europe, but fewer pilgrims than usual because of the war being fought against the Russians in the east. In fact, the issue that had set off the war was the jurisdiction over the Holy Sepulcher, sacred to all Christians as the place where Christ was crucified and entombed, and where He rose from the dead.

I awoke on the morning of the ceremony to the painful din of the beating of drums and the shouts of Moslems parading the streets of Jerusalem. Despite the thick stone walls of my lodgings, the noise reverberated through my body and made me feel uneasy. On my way over to the Finns, we passed a number of these processions. Their manner was as intimidating as the clamor they were making. These religious zealots had clearly worked themselves into a frenzy. The consul's *kawwas* stuck even closer to me than usual to prevent anything untoward from occurring.

The paraders carried green banners inscribed with the Moslem crescent and Arabic texts. A bodyguard, carrying a battle-ax, a spear and a long brassbound gun, accompanied each flag, followed by men with large drums and cymbals. They moved along slowly in the direction of Nebi Musa, a holy place for the Moslems near the Dead Sea, where they believe the tomb of the prophet Moses is located. The consul later explained that the Nebi Musa pilgrimage had been purposefully instituted to coincide with the Christian pilgrimages to the Holy Sepulcher, the arrival of Moslems meant to offset the presence of so many thousands of devout Christians in Jerusalem at one time.

The Moslem processions have strong anti-Christian overtones and sometimes, I was told, they could get extremely violent. Since the war in the Crimea began, the Moslems have become even more antagonistic. The chance of violence breaking out between them and the equally fervid Christian pilgrims in the crowded streets and bazaars through which they drove their processions, was considerable. According to the consul, the authorities always heaved a sigh of relief when these pilgrimages ended peacefully.

Since the consul himself was taken up with other duties that day, I attended the ceremony with Mrs. Finn, the vice-consul Mr. Rogers, and some English travelers who were under Mr. Rogers's care. All of us were, of course, accompanied by the consul's *kawwas*.

On our way through the crowded market and alleyways we carefully avoided trampling on pilgrims camped out along the road. Mr. Rogers explained that in order to be as near to the sepulcher as possible, they take up their places from the afternoon of Holy Friday. The lucky ones spend the night sleeping on the stone floors around the tomb. Those who arrive late on the day of the miracle cannot get beyond the main door.

The rite we were about to observe, according to Mr. Rogers, is of great antiquity, although its origins are obscure. For the Greeks it represents the flame stolen from heaven by Prometheus, and for the Christians the fire that "came down from heaven, and consumed the burnt offering" during Solomon's consecration of the first Jewish Temple. Nonbelievers, however, claim the "miracle" is most probably the result of a simple chemical reaction between two liquids or powders mixed together behind the sealed door of the aedicule.

Christian groups began vying for control of the holy places after the Crusaders conquered Jerusalem in 1099 and the Catholic Church gained control of the sacred sites. The result has been eight hundred years of outright enmity. Which religious group will have the upper hand depends on the political climate and on how much money has passed into the pockets of the authorities. Sometimes the Turks decree in favor of the Catholics, sometimes in favor of the Orthodox. Once they even tried giving two communities rights to the same holy site, telling each that it was to be theirs alone. Apparently, nobody was pleased with the results.

There are also constant provocations and even physical fights within the Orthodox ranks themselves. Like many disputes, the squabbles seem petty and trivial to outsiders. In Bethlehem, for instance, the Greek Orthodox once placed a carpet in front of the Armenian altar. When Armenians came to worship, the Greek Orthodox attacked them for stepping on the rug. For much of the Christian world these issues are as vital as the air they breathe and this is especially true with regard to the Church of the Holy Sepulcher.

When we arrived at the area around the church, there were masses of people. The Christian Arabs were all chanting traditional hymns at the top of their voices accompanied by the sound of the ever-present drums. They had apparently been doing so since eleven o'clock that morning. The din was tremendous.

Inside the building there was a sickly scent of incense, making the already close air even heavier. Every inch of the floors, galleries, corridors and chapels was packed tightly with people. Others were standing on the window ledges and had even climbed up on pillars and the roof scaffolding. Due to the influence of Mrs. Finn and Mr. Rogers, we were allowed into the gallery to witness the ceremony in relative comfort.

As the time for the ceremony drew near, the supplicants began to climb up on each other's shoulders and pray for the fire to come down and save them. The combination of the chaos and lack of air made me feel faint. Mrs. Finn passed me a dampened handkerchief to place over my mouth.

At one o'clock, the chants faded and a tense silence prevailed, charged with the anticipation. A delegation from the local Turkish authorities elbowed its way through the crowd and went down into the tomb. Their role in the ritual was to represent the Romans at the time of Jesus, who, according to tradition, had sealed the tomb with wax so that Jesus's disciples would not steal his body and claim he had risen from the dead. Before sealing the door, according to custom, they entered the tomb, and checked for any hidden source of fire that might make a fraud of the miracle. The Greek Orthodox patriarch then entered the tomb, and the Turks sealed it behind him.

Mr. Rogers explained what would be happening inside the aedicule. The patriarch would kneel in front of the stone on which Christ was laid after his death and say certain prayers, at which point the miracle was meant to occur. A blue light would materialize from the core of the stone – which would kindle oil lamps as well as the patriarch's two candles. The patriarch would then hand the light out to the crowd through a narrow opening in the wall.

As we waited silently in the darkened sanctuary, a fire did, in fact, burst forth from the opening. It lit up the whole church and thousands of eager pilgrims pressed forwards to light their candles. In a frenzy of activity, young local Christians competed with each other to light their candles, vying to be the first to bring them to their churches. Several pilgrims, many of them elderly women from

Greece and Cyprus, carried bundles of tapers – thirty-three tapers to signify the years of Jesus's life – and Russian pilgrims carried tin containers with two funnels at the top to let the air escape.

The worshippers shouted and sometimes wrestled with one another in the attempt to reach the fire with their candles. When they succeeded, they rushed out to the streets to pass on the flames to the thousands of pilgrims anxiously hugging their tapers outside.

The scene was one of frightful confusion with strong violent undertones. Hysterical fanatics rushed around, searing themselves with lighted tapers, in a kind of penance. We were jostled and shoved until for a short time I lost sight of those I had come with. I must admit I was becoming very distressed. The Turkish guards I could see stood there at first doing nothing, with nasty smirks smeared across their faces.

We had expected to hear a roar of exultation resounding in the church when the "miracle" occurred. But immediately after the appearance of the flame, as if the existing bedlam were not sufficient, a disturbance broke out between the Greeks and Armenians. It had apparently been planned in advance with both adversaries stashing stones and sticks behind columns and in darkened crevices. When the mayhem broke loose more weapons were thrown into the church through a window near the Greek convent. My biggest fear at first was that the whole place was going to be set aflame and that since there was only one exit to the church we would all be burned or trampled to death.

Finally, the pasha deigned to leave his seat in the rear gallery and come down to break up the fracas. He and his soldiers only succeeded in finally doing so after he himself received several severe blows to the head, and his secretary had been cut on the hand by a knife. A number of Greeks and Armenians were also wounded as were the commander of the Turkish troops and many of his soldiers.

Mr. Rogers managed with the help of the *kawwas* to get us out of the building. I kept worrying about Mrs. Finn's flowing clothing, afraid her scarf could easily catch on fire. I got a rather bad burn on my lower left arm when a frantic pilgrim brushed her bundle of candles against me. When we finally got away from the church, I was relieved to see that besides a few superficial wounds we were all fine, although naturally quite upset. We returned to the Finns' home to recover.

Mr. Rogers went back later with the consul to allow him to witness the devastation with his own eyes. That evening the consul told us what he had seen.

The square in front of the church was being guarded by Turkish soldiers, he said. Inside, the church was strewn with broken lamps, shards of glass, oil and the tattered remains of many precious religious paintings and church ornaments. Efforts were being made to clean up the debris and return this holiest of places to its former state. The pavement was being washed down and what could be salvaged was being carried away for refurbishment; what needed to be replaced, like the lamps on the walls of the church, was being dealt with. Some Syrian women were chanting hypnotically on the upper gallery.

Mr. Finn talked to a Greek monk who was doing his best to prepare for the evening prayers. He of course blamed the Armenians for the damage and voiced his objections to their presence in the church at any time. Non-Orthodox monks that he talked to volubly denounced the barbarism of both the communities.

And so ended the events of that day. It is a great shame that such partisan squabbles spoil what was meant to be a solemn ritual performed with dignity to invigorate the beliefs of true devotees – for some for the rest of their lives.

PART II

Chapter 11

Rebecca's Arrival in Jerusalem

Leaving New York had been difficult for Rebecca, even though she knew she was doing the right thing. She related to it more as an experiment – dipping her toe into the water – rather than a step she was willing to commit herself to at this point. Her friends were not tuned into her ambivalence and when Yana parted from her as if she would never see her again, Rebecca snapped back, "I'm only going for six months, no big deal." Packing up had given it all an irrevocable feel as well. And putting down poor Elsie was just too painful to think about.

She had spent the last few weeks reading through some of Zara's journals of her years in Jerusalem, as well as letters to her friend Helga, which had somehow been added to the collection. Rebecca felt she had to experience the place firsthand. She brought along some of the material with her. The rest she had sent.

As soon as she landed at Ben Gurion Airport, she immediately felt the energy of the country. During the taxi ride up to Jerusalem, which she shared with several other people, she had some surprisingly intense conversations with the other passengers. She was amazed to see the large number of settlements near Jerusalem. At the entrance to the city they had to battle with a serious traffic jam.

Upon her arrival at the Jerusalem YMCA, where she had reserved a room for the first week, she was greeted by the gentle chimes of carillon bells reverberating from the central tower of the building. Their purity of sound lifted her spirits. According to the hotel clerk, the carillon concert heralded the opening of a ten-day chamber music festival run by the wife of Daniel Barenboim, Elena Bashkirova, a world-famous pianist in her own right. Rebecca soon found herself wrangling for one of the few tickets left for the evening concert.

The concert hall was tastefully decorated with symbols of the three main religions. Rebecca had to make do with a wooden seat at the back between a gnarled-looking old man in a baseball cap who promptly fell asleep and a female music student who could barely contain her excitement from the moment the artists walked on stage. Barenboim himself played with a group of young artists, including his own son, Michael.

Despite her fatigue from the journey, Rebecca thoroughly enjoyed the evening.

She went to sleep that night feeling serene. She was pleased to have a job in this town for at least the next six months, and grateful to Yana for having arranged it.

The next morning she breakfasted alone on the terrace of the Y. The serenity she had been feeling the night before somewhat dissipated in the din of the incessant traffic on King David Street below. At one point, she looked up and saw that the arched roof above her was spattered with old bullet holes. The man at the next table explained they had been left from the War of Independence as a reminder of what had transpired in the country at the time.

He then pointed to the King David Hotel across the street. "That building is famous for having been bombed by right-wing leader Menachem Begin and his friends before the founding of the state. Since then it has hosted many world figures who have come here under the mistaken belief that they can settle the endless conflict in this area with logic and reason." This last statement was accompanied by a derisive guffaw.

After breakfast, Rebecca climbed the winding staircase to the top of the central tower to get a better view of the city. With the help of her guidebook, she identified the Mount of Olives to the east, which Zara had mentioned in her journals, and the new decorative bridge at the entrance to the city to the west. In between, she could see the densely populated city at this time of day filled with people rushing to their chosen destinations. This was far from the desolate town that had greeted Zara upon her arrival, Rebecca thought.

She was anxious to find out how much of Zara's world still existed. After meeting her new boss at the Israel Museum that afternoon, she planned to visit some of the places she had read about in the journals.

Oren Mor was the head curator of the Israel Museum's Youth Wing. He first explained the ins and outs of the place and then informed her she was going to be working on an exhibit on Russian Jewry. Just up her alley. After this rather brief interview, he offered to show her around the Old City.

"But you must be busy," Rebecca protested.

"Actually, it's part of my job to entertain guests."

"Well, if that's the case, how can I refuse!"

Rebecca was flattered by his generosity and attention. She also felt attracted to Oren from the beginning, which surprised her. She had not expected to be interested in someone so soon. For the meantime, she put it down to the romantic air of the city.

Oren was quite ordinary looking – tall, of medium build, with a boyish lock of blond hair lolling over his forehead. He was dressed the way she imagined a kibbutznik would be dressed, in a white cotton shirt, khaki shorts and sandals. As it turned out, he had in fact been one. She soon discovered he was also an expert in almost everything – local art, history, archeology. And, of course, he knew the Bible inside out.

As they entered Jaffa Gate, the sights, sounds and smells over-whelmed Rebecca. She immediately recognized the locale as the one in Elizabeth's drawing. There were still Arab men and women in traditional dress but the square was mostly filled with tourists and taxi drivers hawking for fares.

They stopped at Christ Church, where Zara had spent her first days. "It's now a hospice for travelers," Oren explained. They had a cup of coffee in the peaceful atmosphere of the café away from the noise of the street outside. Rebecca fell silent for a few minutes. Oren ventured to ask her what she was thinking about.

"I'm trying to imagine what this place was like in the nine-teenth century." Rebecca began to tell Oren about Zara and her journals and letters and about how they had drawn her to the country. The historian in him perked up and Rebecca promised to show him some of them.

From there they continued to the Western Wall via the Arme-nian Quarter. Though Rebecca had seen pictures of the Western Wall, her sense of what it would look like had been influenced by Zara's writings and she instinctively expected to feel the claus-trophobia that Zara had experienced when she first visited there. Instead, she found herself looking over a spacious, well-cared-for plaza with armed guards posted at all entrances. There were only a few religious Jews and tourists praying or wandering around the plaza.

"This isn't at all what I imagined. Zara's journals describe a very different place."

"The Moslem houses in front of the Wall were destroyed shortly after the Six-Day War and replaced with this large segre-gated plaza. The Jewish Quarter has been rebuilt and modernized. But, believe me, the religious fervor remains."

Oren went on to tell her about the confrontations that had taken place there in the last century, how the Jews had been forced to leave the Jewish Quarter at the end of the War of Independence and about the excitement when it returned to Israeli hands in 1967.

"Much of the territory captured in the Six-Day War is still in dispute and many have grave doubts about how wise it was to keep it after the war." Rebecca was not entirely ignorant of the conflicts in the country but, for now, she just wanted to take in the atmosphere of the place. She let Oren continue without commenting.

"The Jews praying here now, although in appearance not very different from those who prayed here when your relative lived here, are far from the obsequious, wretched Jews of that time. They consider themselves the masters of the place. Together with this self-assurance comes a strong statement of retribution for the humiliations they suffered here for centuries. Many of the secular and non-ultra-Orthodox religious Jews fear they will take over all of Jerusalem within the next twenty-five years."

"I'm not sure Zara would have been comfortable with their attitude either," Rebecca answered.

"Not that the Jewish control over the area has been entirely successful," Oren continued. "The Temple Mount on the other side of the Wall is still controlled by a Moslem council called the Waqf. Jews are allowed there only as visitors these days and Moslem Arabs demonstrate regularly on the mount, sometimes violently."

They sat on a low wall watching the people come and go, occasionally being accosted for contributions to various Jewish charities.

Rebecca was still preoccupied with her aunt's visit here. "It may sound strange but I think my aunt's first visit to the Wall was her way of breaking with her Orthodox religious background. I believe she felt she had fulfilled her promise of coming here and now she could move on in a new direction."

"That's possible. But you know many secular Jews also have a strong attachment to the Wall. It represents a significant part of Jewish history. I know that for me it's very important, even though I'm not religious at all."

They sat for a while longer, each lost in thought.

"You know, Oren, I'm only Jewish on my father's side, which makes me officially not Jewish at all. One of the reasons I've come here is to explore that part of me, to see how great a role I want my Judaism to play in my life."

"There are many different ways of practicing Judaism. I can help you look into them if you like and then you'll make your own decision."

"Thank you, I'd appreciate that."

When they had had enough, they wandered back through the winding roads of the Christian Quarter. Oren bought some Turkish delight for them to enjoy while walking and some local spices for the meal he promised to cook her the next evening. They stopped at a restaurant for Jerusalem-style humus.

Rebecca could feel herself moving into a different mind-set. Layers of defenses were rapidly peeling away. She was overcome with a strange sensation of déjà vu, which at first she attributed to Zara's influence. But when she thought about it more deeply she felt there was something indefinably primal about it.

On her way back to the hotel, she absentmindedly tugged at a few eucalyptus leaves leaning over the sidewalk from one of the yards. She rubbed them between her fingers and pressed them to her nose to get a whiff of the pungent odor. As she sat now in the garden café of the Y, it still lingered on her hands.

Chapter 12

Zara Begins Her Life in Jerusalem

April 20, 1856

Dear Helga,

The holiday season is now over, the pilgrims have returned to wherever they came from and Jerusalem has settled back into its daily routine. I have begun to consider my options for the foreseeable future. There is no doubt I will stay here at least for the next six months. I am enamored with the place. So my first order of business has been to find somewhere to live.

As far as location is concerned, after some consideration I've opted to take a house near the Damascus Gate, in the Moslem Quarter. It is more exotic than the Christian part of the city and although I dearly love the Finns, I want to put some distance between myself and their missionary activities.

I am also not keen on living in the Jewish Quarter. Even though those people are of my faith, I feel I have little in common with them. I cannot tolerate the degradation they allow themselves to be subjected to nor can I accept their parasitical existence. I suppose living in America for so long has given me a greater pride in my own worth.

Although some have tried to deter me from the dangers I might expose myself to far from my own kind, strangely enough I am unafraid. I had a charming conversation with a rather eccentric Englishwoman who has lived in the area for a few years now. Her name is Carrie. She maintains that for her, the fact that there are no Europeans in the Moslem Quarter is a point strongly in its favor. Usually, she says, the only people visible during the day there are black slaves lolling outside their masters' homes. The day is punctuated mainly by the cry of the muezzin and on a sleepless night its soothing wail can provide welcome company when you are alone.

On the other hand, she says, in the Christian Quarter people rush along quickly without looking left or right, completely oblivious to their surroundings. When one sees them at large, they have a strained, sober look about them, much like that of the squeezed lemons that lie on the saucers of their daily teacups. Their clothes are spartan, and lack the fluid movement of the Moslem dress that floats past you in their quarter. According to her, the Moslem's strong sense of self-respect makes him proceed at a more dignified pace.

I was enchanted by this romantic depiction of the Moslem Quarter and have decided to give it a try. What worries me most, which is quite silly I know, is how I will communicate with the servant I will need to take on, at least in the beginning. Elizabeth assures me that sign language will suffice as long as I show patience and understanding if, as she says, "I should at first, for example, be served my afternoon tea in a soup tureen rather than a cup." As I am not much inclined to taking afternoon tea that shouldn't be a problem.

Since Elizabeth had lived in the quarter herself with her brother Walter when she first arrived, she was sympathetic to my choice and has been quite helpful in getting me started. I hoped to get a decent place for one thousand piasters, with the option of extending the rental for another half year at least. I will have to pay for the whole six months in advance, which is going to make me quite short of money for the next little while. I'm counting on your skill at negotiating with the Times to see me through, dear Helga.

Through James's consular connections, I was shown around the area by a Christian Arab acquaintance of theirs. When I

opened my door to him on the day and hour we had fixed,
I found myself facing a distinctive-looking young man. His
already large stature was augmented by a turban, under which
peered out a pair of intelligent, black eyes. Despite his servile
demeanor, it was evident he was quick and clever and could
teach me a thing or two about life in the Holy City.

He dressed well but his clothes were all in dark colors.
Quite out of character with the rest of his attire were his bright
red shoes. Elizabeth later explained that under Moslem rule
Christians were forbidden to wear brightly colored clothing.
But since the Egyptian period, some of this had changed and
these shoes were most likely a statement of his newfound
independence.

Instead of the aggressive weaponry of the dragomen, a
metal inkhorn protruded out of my agent's waistband. He also
carried three bunches of large, clumsy keys.

"Good morning, madam. My name is Abu Dahud. I will be
your guide today," he said when I opened the door. "I am well
acquainted with the area and the people. You can rely on me. If
there is a suitable house to be found here for you, I will find it.
Please follow me." And without further ado, we set off.

The houses in the Moslem Quarter, I learned, are rented
out by Moslem effendis, the heads of noble Arab families who
have lived in Jerusalem for generations – a status they are very
proud of. However, since their financial circumstances have
worsened of late, they have been forced to rent them. Usually,
they manage to let them for large sums, as they are quite in
demand. But Abu Dahud assured me it was possible to bring
the price down once they realized the potential tenant was
serious and deemed suitable.

We walked through narrow alleys between high walls
punctuated here and there by a low doorway. The first place
we entered was owned by a man called Suleiman, named for
the famous sixteenth-century Ottoman ruler, Suleiman the
Magnificent.

Abu Dahud banged the knocker on the door vigorously. After a few minutes Suleiman himself opened the door. Despite his impressive name, Suleiman was not much to look at. He seemed to have just woken up, although it was already long past ten in the morning. His hair was tousled, thick and long and he had a two-day growth of beard. He was sloppily appareled in a long striped house dress, known by the Arabs as a *jellabiya*, with not-too-recent food stains running down the front. He led us into a reception room which was quite bare except for a rather worn settee in the corner with a small threadbare rug in front of it. He spoke a few words to Abu Dahud and pointed to the three rooms off of the central room. He then sat down on the settee to wait for us.

Abu Dahud led me through the three rooms. All of them were small, dark and poorly kept. We then went up a stone staircase to a small terrace surrounded by high walls. The terrace was empty of furniture and offered no view of the surrounding area.

I immediately knew that this was not what I was looking for and informed Abu Dahud. We went back downstairs to find our host spread out on the sofa with his eyes closed. He sat up grudgingly upon our arrival. When Abu Dahud politely explained to him that his client was not interested in the place, giving the excuse that it was too large for me, the man shrugged and led us indifferently to the door.

When we were outside the house, Abu Dahud apologized profusely for bringing me to this place. He said the father of this man had been an important figure in the city but since his death the son had wasted his time gambling away his inheritance and had obviously let the place and himself run down considerably.

As we waited outside the door of a second house, Abu Dahud told me a bit about the owner. He pointed out that he was a respected member of the Moslem community who was traveling to Europe to take care of his frail health. When a servant finally opened the door, we passed through the entrance, bending slightly to avoid banging our heads on the marble lintel.

This house was in much better condition than the first one and as we were shown around the rooms I was quite taken by the place. After we had seen the rooms on the main floor the servant led us down to a lower level to show us the kitchen. On our way we passed a small room in which was huddled a group of well-dressed, bejeweled women and children who were very excited to see us. Abu Dahud explained that this was the harem of the owner of the house and that he had probably tried to hide them away while we there. The woman who seemed to be the main wife looked quite young and greatly overweight, a kind of Oriental house cat. My agent assured me that of course the harem would be going off to Europe with the owner. I was still appalled at the thought that, however well cared for they were, these women were virtually the property of one man. I asked to leave.

Abu Dahud unquestioningly led me out of the house and we continued on to the next place. We proceeded to what was one of the finer streets of the Moslem Quarter. The houses were a bit dilapidated but the area, it was clear, had once been quite splendid. As we walked, Abu Dahud pointed out a doorway built in alternate rows of red and black stone. He explained that this was the style of the Mameluke period.

I was ashamed to say I was not at all familiar with the Mameluke period so I kept that to myself. I often feel very ignorant around people like Abu Dahud. I have so much to learn about this place and its history.

The particular house we were heading towards was owned by a Moslem who was planning an extended visit to his family in Egypt. I had no argument with that. In response to our knock the door was opened by a tall, bony-looking servant who showed us into a pleasant little courtyard, most of which was shaded by a vine trellis. I was grateful for the protection since the afternoon heat was beginning to affect me. As we waited,

I sat down at the edge of a well and ran my fingers through its surprisingly cool water. A shuttered door hid the surrounding rooms from view.

The slave soon returned and took us through the door to a reasonably sized antechamber. He opened a latticed window, which offered us a pleasant view of the surrounding area.

There were only two rooms off the antechamber but they were quite spacious and spotlessly clean. We then walked back out to the courtyard, over to the other side of the house and up a stone staircase to a third room, which was quite cool and secluded from the surrounding houses. We could see from its small window a view of the Jaffa Gate area. Outside the room was a pleasant little terrace with a small wooden table and a few chairs. I could easily imagine myself and whatever friends I might make during my stay sitting around here on a warm summer evening. The servant then led us downstairs to a tiny little kitchen and a small space that was meant to serve as the servant's quarters.

The house was smaller than what I had planned to rent but it was quaint and I was quite happy with it. I whispered this to Abu Dahud and made it clear to him that I was definitely interested in renting it. Abu Dahud assured me that there was enough water in the house cistern for the year, a matter I had not even considered. He said a few words to the slave, who directed us back to the antechamber, bowed and walked off.

The owner, who had apparently been waiting in a nearby café, soon arrived. He was a tall, meticulously groomed middle-aged man. He wore a light-colored robe over a long silk vest and wide Oriental trousers, cinched at the waist with a cashmere shawl. On his head he had a bright red tarbush with a white turban wrapped around it and on his feet he wore Oriental slippers as brightly colored as Abu Dahud's shoes. As he made a deep bow on his entrance, the top of his tarbush was exposed to us.

Abu Dahud introduced me to our host. I learned that he

was called Amjad Effendi. We were then led to a beautifully upholstered blue divan that encompassed almost the entire antechamber. The effendi removed his slippers and seated himself cross-legged on a rug in the corner. We also removed our shoes, and made ourselves comfortable on the opposite side of the divan. The effendi then bowed again to each of us individually and asked us politely as to the state of our health. Abu Dahud answered for both of us and made a similarly polite enquiry about his health. The owner gave a vague response and then there was silence.

Abu Dahud sat erect, his hands folded on his knees and covered as much as possible by his sleeves. His eyes were lowered most of the time. The effendi, on the other hand, seemed quite at ease. When he finally spoke, Abu Dahud answered respectfully, agreeing with everything he said.

After another short interval of silence an intricate ritual followed during which we were served lemonade and coffee in succession by two different servants. A third servant then brought in long pipes for each of the men. I, too, was offered one but I refused. The servant then withdrew, closing the latticed door behind him. Abu Dahud began the negotiations slowly.

"I understand you are planning on visiting your family in Egypt in the near future."

"*Inshallah*, please God."

"When does your honor plan to leave?"

"After Ramadan."

"And your honor intends to rent out his property over that period?"

"That is true."

Abu Dahud paused for a long moment. Then he said, pointing to me, "This American woman, a dear friend of the English consul and his wife, is looking for a house." Abu Dahud continued to proceed with the negotiations until he successfully brought the effendi around to the subject of money.

Abu Dahud offered 750 piasters, with the hope of getting to the 1000 piasters I was willing to pay. They proceeded delicately until the sum of 900 piasters had been offered by Abu Dahud. The effendi then said that since we had been sent by the venerable consul, we should have it for the desired 1000 piasters.

He then went back to puffing on his pipe as if to close the matter. Abu Dahud sat for a minute more and then rose to leave, once again making a deep salaam. I did the same and we both backed cautiously out of the room. The effendi remained behind.

"So did I get the place?" I asked when we were back in the courtyard. I was still unclear of what had transpired even though Abu Dahud had managed to translate the significant issues for me during the transaction.

"Yes, and for the exact price you wanted to pay."

I wanted to kiss Abu Dahud but that, of course, I knew was entirely inappropriate.

"Is that all there is to it?"

"Arabs are a very proud people. Their word is final. The deal is completed. The house is yours," my mediator explained.

I took one more glance around me to reassure myself about my decision. I was very pleased and thanked Abu Dahud profusely for his help. The effendi emerged at that exact moment as if he had been listening at the door. He took leave of us graciously and promised the house would be ready in ten days.

And so I have found me a home, Helga. I'm very excited. Remember, there is always a room for you if ever you decide to visit, with views you'll find enchanting.

Your friend,

Zara

Chapter 13

Letters

June 1856

Dear Zara,

I was very happy to receive your letter and the article about your visit to the Holy Sepulcher. I always knew you had a way with words but your descriptions are so vivid, I feel like I am right there with you. I immediately showed the article to my friend at the New York Times and he was very impressed. The paper decided to publish it almost immediately and the responses have been more than enthusiastic.

I have enclosed a copy of the printed article as well as a contract for ten more pieces! They are offering you quite a handsome sum, which I'm sure will only increase with time. The byline will remain anonymous – "A Traveler to the Holy Land" – until you decide what you want to do about that. The mystery of it all has turned you into a popular topic of conversation around here: Who is this person? Why is she there? And so on and so forth. I find it hard to control myself. But I also must tell you that I have a feeling the boys are suspicious, so you might feel the need to censor yourself accordingly or at least give them some idea of what is going on.

I am also enclosing a letter addressed to you and brought to me by a government official. He made me swear not to open it and to make sure it got safely into your hands. I was dying of curiosity but I have kept my promise and am sending it on in pristine condition.

Things here are more or less the same. The main issue of the presidential elections this year is, of course, slavery. The Republicans have run a campaign calling for the repeal of the hated Kansas-Nebraska Act in order to oppose the extension of slavery into the territories, but Buchanan hasn't managed to corner enough support to really do anything.

Everyone here is fine. I miss you so much. I feel that I don't have anyone to talk to anymore, at least about things that matter. The mail boats are so slow that by the time I get a letter from you months have passed. But please keep writing. I can't wait to read about your next adventure. Don't despair and get as much as you can out of this special challenge you have given yourself.

Love,
Helga

An excerpt from a letter to Zara's sons, July 1856:

My dearest boys,

I hope this letter finds you and your families well. I miss you all very much. I felt I should tell you a little of what I'm up to here so you won't be too surprised when you hear of it from others.

I am finding life here very difficult but also extremely interesting. In order to keep body and soul together – I know you were worried about that, Isaac – I have begun writing travelogues for the new newspaper, the New York Times. If you haven't guessed yet, I am the "Traveler to the Holy Land." So you can keep up with my meanderings through those pieces as well as my letters. Please don't worry about me as I am in good hands. The Finns take great care of me and I am getting to know many new and fascinating people.

I also wanted to tell you that I have moved into a place of my own in the Moslem Quarter. You should continue to write "Via Trieste" on your letters. Don't forget, because otherwise letters can get bogged down in the Ottoman mail system, which is worth an article on its own....

Chapter 14

A Literary Soirée

July 1856

Dear Helga,

I hope all is well with you. Enclosed you will find my next article for the Times based on my experiences of the past few weeks.

The community of foreigners is very small in this city. Everyone seems to know everyone else. I was invited by Elizabeth to a literary evening sponsored by the Jerusalem Literary Society, a society established by the Finns several years ago. It is supposed to be limited to only Protestants, but Elizabeth has made an exception in my case.

Since I've been living on my own for a while and am still finding it difficult to adjust to the everyday life of the city, I was glad of the opportunity to be among friendly faces for a few hours.

At this particular meeting, the subject was Charles Dickens's new novel *David Copperfield*. Even though I had not yet read it, I enjoyed hearing the various points of view discussed. The focus was the social issues that Dickens so vividly presents. There were several comparisons drawn to the unfortunate lives of many Moslem, Jewish and Christian children in the Holy Land. I was shocked to hear about the terrible situation of these children here.

Elizabeth introduced me to a number of other English-speaking foreigners, many of whom have recently come to the country and are here for various purposes and lengths of time.

They included three Prussians, two Danes, one Swede and
one Bavarian. Among those living more permanently in the
country – as permanent as anyone can hope to live here – was
a man by the name of John Meshullam, a local hotel owner,
and his twenty-five-year-old son Peter, both of whom are deeply
involved in missionary activities in the country. I found them
both rather intense.

One of the people I managed to talk with in more depth
at this gathering was a Miss Cooper, a benevolent and brave
English lady who runs a charitable house to help the poor
Jewish women of Jerusalem. It is called the Jewesses' Institution
and has been in operation since 1848. Many of the women who
work there are widows with families, for whom the money they
earn is their major source of income. I was impressed by her
efforts to provide these women with a vocational education,
especially considering the strong opposition she encounters
from the Jewish rabbinical establishment.

She asked me if I would be interested in volunteering at her
institution. It sounded like something I should do and I found it
difficult to beg off. But in the end I did, claiming I still needed
some time to settle in, which is true. I promised to reconsider
the suggestion a few months from now.

But the most interesting individuals I was introduced
to were two German priests, Conrad Schick and Ferdinand
Christian Palmer, who are living in the House of Industry, an
institution sponsored by the London Jews' Society. This society
has given support to the two priests since 1850, after the
German Protestant Church virtually abandoned them to their
own resources. Schick and Palmer have been in the country
ten years and are presently teaching Jewish men a trade in the
hope, of course, of converting them to Christianity.

One of Conrad's new students accompanied them to the
soirée. He is a young convert named Moses Wilhelm Shapira,
who is living in the compound of the Christ Church and has
also been befriended by the Finns. The young man explained to

me that he had adopted the name Wilhelm to honor Frederick William IV, the king of Prussia. He's an average-looking young man with light blue eyes and brown hair. His moustache and beard cover full lips, which made him look as if they were in a constant pout. He explained that he had come to the country with his grandfather, who had died en route. I shivered when I heard another story of an old man dying on his way to the Holy Land. My experience seems to have been more the rule than the exception. He has been searching for his father, who left his family behind in Poland to come here ten years ago and has never been heard of since. The young man appears to me a little strange and very bewildered. It looks like Schick has taken him under his wing, as no Jew would come near him since he is a convert.

At the end of the evening Reverend Schick approached me with a very interesting proposal.

"Mrs. Rubens," he said, "I hope you will not consider me too – what you say – forward. I consulted with Elizabeth and she suggested I talk with you."

"What is it, Reverend Schick? I'm sure I'll be glad to help you in any way I can," I answered.

"Well, you see, Mrs. Rubens, I am connected deeply with the British in my work here now and I find it necessary to improve my English. Is there any possibility you could find time to teach me?"

I was at first taken aback. "I must tell you, Reverend," I said, "that, first of all, your English seems quite adequate and, secondly, I have no experience as an English teacher. English is not even my native tongue."

"How you say it, Mrs. Rubens? All is relative. Compared to me, I think your English is excellent."

I hesitated for a few minutes, examining this otherworldly man more closely. He seemed so sympathetic and kind that I couldn't refuse. "Perhaps we could give it a try," I said. "If it doesn't work out, no harm done."

"Exactly my feelings, madam," he answered, very pleased.

This kind of pastime seemed much more suited to my temperament than working with the poor, at least at this point in my stay here. I also saw it as an opportunity to get to know this remarkable gentleman better and to have something to occupy my time besides self-pity.

And so has begun what I think will be a second meaningful friendship for me here in the Holy Land. I have met with Conrad several times since and we have become good friends. He's an extremely modest, reserved man and speaks softly, with the shyness of a truly religious soul. He is small in stature and looks rather fragile. I understand that since his arrival in the country he has fought with illness frequently, but this has not prevented him from taking on a variety of projects.

Our initial encounters with the country were quite similar in many ways, so we had these common experiences to share in our first conversations. I told him a little about my background and about how I ended up in Jerusalem. After a while, he opened up to me and told me about himself. For him it was an opportunity to make use of his English and I was fascinated by what he had to say. After each meeting, I carefully recorded everything in my personal journal – with some corrections in the English, of course. Conrad has given me permission to submit his story as my next article to the Times, which I am enclosing here. I hope they will consider it worthy of publication.

Let me know what you think of it.

Your dearest friend,

Zara

THE STORY OF CONRAD SCHICK
As Told to a Traveler to the Holy Land
Jerusalem, July 1856

I know you will find it hard to believe but my first job in this country, along with my colleague Christian Palmer, was selling and fixing cuckoo clocks, an item much in demand in Jerusalem when we arrived. In preparation for our service here, Palmer and I had learned the trade of watchmaking in a famous center for manufacturing cuckoo clocks in Schwarzwald, Germany. The head of the missionary that sent us here, Friedrich Spittler, believed this would be a useful profession for us and one that could sustain us until we could establish our mission here. And for a while it did.

My connection to Spittler goes back a few years. His mission is the largest mission in Basel and I had wanted to study there when I moved to that city as a very young man. At the time, however, Spittler had recommended I "go up the mountain," as he called it, to a new institution called the Pilgrim's Mission.

My life at the Pilgrim's Mission was not that satisfying. The living conditions were poor, the teachings not very serious and I was required to do a lot of hard physical work which was very difficult for me. One of the more interesting tasks they gave me, though, was to construct a model of the *Ohel Moed* – the Tabernacle in which the Jews assembled to worship God in the desert. It was used to illustrate the Bible stories for the town's schoolchildren. The pleasure I got out of doing this work gave me the inspiration to make many more models since then and I continue to do so to this day.

I have always been fascinated by the Bible stories. As a child I was very feeble and delicate. I grew up in a small rural town in southwest Germany called Bitz where even young children were expected to do farm work. I tried to do my share but I was so weak my mother often worried I might not make it to the end of the day. I spent a lot of time in my room. While other children were out playing in the street, I sat there reading the Bible. I also did a lot of drawing and painting, which is probably the reason I enjoy doing these models so much.

At the end of my schooling I was apprenticed to a metalworker in a town near Stuttgart for three years. I found the work difficult but I got courage from the strong religious atmosphere of the place. It was an opportunity for me to meet many inspiring religious men. I began to think of becoming a man of the cloth myself. But before I could act on my dream I became very ill and was taken home again to be nursed by my mother.

When I recovered, I made a renewed effort to ply my trade as a metalworker but my heart was not in it. After wandering around for a while I found a job in a metal workshop in Basel. But I was still dissatisfied. The religious life in the city was even more intense than what I had experienced in the town near Stuttgart and this is what drew me. It inspired me to again try to realize my dream of becoming a man of the cloth. That was when I went to talk to Spittler. He could see that I was sincere about my religious beliefs and so found me a place at the Pilgrim's Mission.

I was to encounter Spittler again a year later. Our next meeting turned out to be even more momentous for me. One of my brothers at the Pilgrim's Mission fell ill one winter day. I was in town at the time and was instructed to take Spittler up to see him. Spittler felt responsible for this new mission since he had sent so many young men like me to study there. While we were making our way there on a snowy winter's day, Spittler told me about his plans to send students from the Pilgrim's Mission to work as social workers and preachers among German immigrants in America. I told him that I was not really that interested in doing this kind of work. Spittler decided to try a different approach with me and said that he was also looking for a missionary to serve in Jerusalem. I immediately responded that I would gladly be willing to take on such a challenge but added that, as Jesus had sent out his envoys two at a time, I too would like another brother to come along with me. And that was how I got to know Christian Palmer, a dear, kind, generous soul who has seen me through some of the worst times I have had here in the Holy Land.

After we finished our watchmaking training, Palmer and I set off for the Holy Land. The journey over was horrendous. When we finally arrived I was completely incapacitated. For a few months Palmer took care of all our needs. He rented us a house in the Christian Quarter and began familiarizing himself with the city. After observing the conditions of the locals and evaluating our own circumstances he wrote a long letter to Spittler describing in detail the miserable lives of the people in the city, especially the Jews, and also hinting at our own situation, hoping to get us more assistance.

Samuel Gobat, a Swiss-born, German-speaking Anglican minister who had recently assumed the post of Anglican bishop of Jerusalem, was made aware of our presence. He was appalled by our living conditions. He knew Spittler from Germany so he decided to write him a letter of his own.

Spittler's reaction to these missives was to send out a large shipment of dismantled cuckoo clocks which we were supposed to assemble and sell. In the beginning our clocks caused quite a stir in Jerusalem and we were able to improve our financial situation considerably. But neither Palmer nor I was satisfied with the state of affairs. This was not what we had come to do in the Holy Land. What is more, eventually the enthusiasm for our clocks abated and we again found ourselves in dire straits.

Bishop Gobat followed our progress closely and when he saw in the winter, for example, that both of us were seriously ill from the cold, he ordered an iron heater for us from England at his own expense. In general, the bishop has greatly eased our stay here. He and his wife have taken care of us as if we were their own children.

The most useful contact I made during this period was with the mufti of Jerusalem, who approached me to teach his son the art of watchmaking. I agreed to do so happily as I saw it as an opportunity to make contact with some of the local youth. After a while, the mufti's son, as well as a number of other young men in the city, started working for us as gardeners in the small plot of land near our home where we grew vegetables for our personal use. Later, they also became teachers in our modest school.

Palmer and I had become very close during this first difficult period in the country. We lived very simply. As a further means of keeping down our expenses we had also been forbidden to marry, which made our lives even lonelier and more miserable.

Nevertheless, we did our best to get to know the local converts. To this end, Palmer had learned quite a bit of Arabic. I, unfortunately, found learning the language much harder. Spittler sent out two more missionaries to help us and we managed to gather together a group of Arab boys large enough to form a class. It was not easy to educate these boys. They were quite illiterate and incapable of organized thought. We also had a lot of opposition from the Greek Orthodox and Catholic churches which were afraid we would convert our pupils to Protestantism. In the end, they came one day and dragged the boys out by force. It was quite a horrific scene.

As a result of our failure, Palmer and I became very disheartened. We didn't know what to do next. We realized we needed more significant moral and financial backing if we were going to make our mark in this city. We finally decided to leave Spittler's patronage and join the English institutions. This seemed to be the only way we could serve the Protestant Church and improve our living conditions. Another advantage of working for the English was that we would have the diplomatic backing of the British Consulate, which was quite a weighty consideration.

So in November 1850, I moved to the English House of Industry to take over the supervision of trade education there. Soon after, Palmer became a teacher in Gobat's school on Mount Zion.

And this is where we are today. It has been a long and difficult journey for both of us till now. There has been many a day we thought we would not survive, either because of physical weakness, fatigue, hunger or despair. But we have learned to love this country with all our hearts and we are doing our best to help the people here and change what it is possible to change.

Chapter 15

Settling In

An excerpt from a letter to Helga, August 1856:

...I finally feel that I've settled into my new home. On my second week in the neighborhood, I bumped into that eccentric Englishwoman who had encouraged me to live in the Moslem Quarter. She has advised me on how to deal with the servant I've taken on and has helped me set up my home in a way suitable to both my lifestyle and the climate.

She has turned out to be quite an interesting person. Her full name is Carrie Smith. She came over from England about five years ago out of curiosity, having had no former ties to the country at all. I soon discovered that she was really an American from Chicago. Her mother was English and when Carrie was ten the family moved to England.

She apparently was quite a bohemian in London in her time and has moved here to escape the reputation that has prevented her from moving on with her life. She has mothered one illegitimate child who is now grown up and who, after attending Oxford, has become a professor of Far Eastern studies at her alma mater.

Carrie and I have tea together almost every afternoon. Well, at least she has tea and I have coffee. She drinks her tea like the Russians, slurping it up through a lump of sugar between her teeth, which reminds me of my grandfather. She also has two rotted front teeth as a result, as he did, although his had been replaced by gold fillings back in Russia.

We talk about our lives and laugh a lot together. I think she is the only person I ever really laugh with these days. At least twice a week we go shopping in the market. I've become intoxicated by the colors and aromas. But the smells and sights of the fragrant herbs and spices are offset by the revolting appearance and odor of sheep carcasses hanging out of the meat shops and the stench of sewage flowing freely down the streets.

Often we come back with some new exotic vegetable we had never encountered before. Fortunately, they are all familiar to my servant, Aya, who manages to cook up a tasty concoction with whatever we bring.

From time to time we buy a scarf or a light, flowing blouse, or an Arab-style dress with striking Bedouin embroidery. When we get home with our booty, we immediately try everything on, prancing around in front of the mirror. One day Carrie is Scheherazade, keeping danger at bay with seductive stories – and believe me she has a few – and the next I'm Bathsheba, tempting David down from the rooftop with my beauty. Aya is shocked by us. No doubt, we two middle-aged matrons must look rather ridiculous in our efforts to emulate the mysteries of the enigmatic sirens of the East.

But occasionally we have conversations that are more serious. Now that I am ensconced here, I am continually questioning why at all I have made this move.

"What has brought you here?" I asked Carrie one day. "And, even more to the point, what keeps you here?"

"I guess it started with all those Bible stories I was brought up on, as with so many of the people who come here. And, of course, I was escaping my past. And then, after living here a while, it became so absorbing I couldn't leave."

She soaked up some of the eggplant and garlic mixture Aya had prepared for us with a wedge of pita and stuffed it into her mouth before continuing. "In England, all people ever talk about are their gardens, their servants, the weather and other people's boring lives. Here life is so precarious, so precious. It seems to have less value, on one hand, and on the other hand is so much dearer because of the dangers one is always encountering. Not everyone can survive, though. The weather is unbearable for long periods of the year and disease is rampant. Even if you can overcome these difficulties, the weight of the city itself bears down on you. Many a soul has lost his or her mind here and hardly a day goes by without a story about a person whose life has been cut short by just living in this city.

"But those of us who survive are passionate about the place. People of all religions come here to convert and be converted, archeologists are enthusiastic to dig up the past, researchers delve into its long and convoluted history, diplomats do what they can to grab a portion of it for their own country and even misfits like me stay on here for years because we just can't live anywhere else.

"There is no place like Jerusalem. You walk around a corner and you don't know what, or whom, you'll come across. Every day is a lesson in survival. Every day you feel history is being made somehow.

"Take your friends the Finns, for example. They're making some enormous changes here, especially for your people. But not many Europeans really understand what they're doing."

"I suppose you're right." It was good for me to hear Carrie talk; she had put into words a lot of the exhilaration I had been feeling since I arrived here. But nevertheless I had my doubts. "I'm still not sure of the purpose of my life here," I said. "I've given up so much for it. Yet I still behave as if I'm staying forever, as if I have no control over my fate. But I can't imagine ever being anything but an outsider. Of course, I never really felt I belonged anywhere else I've lived till now either."

Carrie answered in her typically iconoclastic manner. "Being outsiders, or *faranji*s, as we're derogatively called by the locals, sometimes gives us the most interesting perspective. Not that anyone here really belongs, not the Turks, the English, the

Germans, the Russians, or even the Jews. The only ones who feel at home are the Arabs who have been here for generations, but if all those who come here keep interfering with them as they do – trying to convert them, take advantage of them economically, give them a bit of political power to pacify them – then the Arabs too will eventually lose their way and won't even feel they belong in their own land."

The more Carrie talks, the less sure of myself I become. She's so brazenly confident, she isn't even aware of the reservations of others. Nor am I sure that her romantic view of the Arabs makes her an accurate judge of their role in the history of the city. "I just don't know if I can live with the uncertainty of the place. And I'm not sure I have enough reasons to try," I told her.

"Don't worry. You will. I can feel it."

So ended our conversation, but not my doubts....

Chapter 16

Daily Life

November 1856

Dearest Helga,

Time is flying by. I am beginning to feel like a permanent fixture in the hustle and bustle of this oh-so-complicated town. My life has taken on a rhythm of its own. I spend the early mornings at home with Aya dealing with domestic matters and then I set out on my daily adventures. Sometimes it's merely to do some shopping in the market, sometimes to spend time with Carrie, and sometimes to have tea with Elizabeth and hear about what is going on in the city. You can never consider what Elizabeth has to tell you as idle gossip, as it's always pitched on a much higher plane. But mostly I do research or interviews for my latest article.

In the evenings I find myself spending most of my time with Carrie, Conrad, Palmer and their student, the rather obstreperous "Wilhelm" Moses Shapira. Occasionally we are joined by the younger Meshullam, Peter, when he isn't taken up with his father's farming projects. Often the Finns are busy so I invite this motley collection of expatriates over for dinner and we sit around the fireplace and pass a few hours together. Sometimes there is some tension between Carrie and Peter or Shapira. She has little patience for either of them. One she considers a sadist and the other a criminal. Conrad usually manages to keep things under control with his civilized manner. So for the most part, we get along and find a lot to talk about.

Conrad's keen interest in the history of the city has infected us all. He is deep into archeological research and constantly busy producing his wooden models of various religious sites with the help of his students. They are considered by many experts to be highly accurate replicas, and foreign historians consult with him regularly.

The one most bitten by Conrad's archeology bug, though, is Wilhelm. We all attended the opening of his shop in the Christian Quarter, where he sells the usual religious trinkets to the tourists as well as ancient pots he acquires from Arab farmers. He seems to be doing quite well. But Carrie is not the only one with doubts about him. Conrad, too, is becoming increasingly suspicious of his activities. It turns out that Wilhelm has joined forces with a Christian Arab potter named Selim al-Khouri, and Conrad has told me in confidence that he believes they are producing fake artifacts and selling them as real at higher and higher prices.

Despite these friendships, my interests and some very exciting adventures, I often feel very lonely, without any real direction. I miss my children. I miss the more secure life in America. And I miss you, my dear friend.

I also find it difficult to watch the suffering of so many of the people around me. Although life has always been difficult in this city, the recent period of drought has created even more extreme poverty. It took me a while to realize what was really going on around me. The streets are crowded with beggars in the most abject rags. Thousands of souls are dependent upon charity for subsistence. Proud Arab farmers have been reduced to begging for bread and devouring the refuse of the vegetable market. Sometimes it's distressing just to walk down the street amid all this misery. Only in the last little while have things begun to slowly improve.

What saves me is my work. As a writer, I get to meet many interesting people, from Bedouin sheiks to English and German dignitaries, to Jews making their way here, not to die, but to revitalize the country. I have even met royalty. Prince Alfred, Queen Victoria's second son, stayed with the Finns recently. They became close friends.

A few weeks ago Carrie and I were invited to the opening of the American Consulate. While there I was approached by an official to prepare detailed reports for them on the subjects I am working on – for a handsome fee, I might add. It seems to me, however, to be a quagmire I don't want to sink into. I have told them I don't consider myself qualified to do such work and that all I have to say is written in my articles for the New York Times, which I know they get regularly.

Please write soon and let me know what you think. Hope all is well with you.

Love,
Zara

Chapter 17

The Finns

An excerpt from a letter to Helga, March 1857:

…My dear friends, the Finns, never cease to be a source of amazement to me. Besides dealing with James's extensive consular duties they have also taken upon themselves to gainfully employ as many Jews as they can. This way these unfortunate people will have to live less and less off of the handouts sent to them from abroad, which have apparently greatly diminished since the war in Crimea.

It took me a while to realize that the Finns' efforts to help the Jews was probably one of the more fascinating stories I could tell. Little did I know at the time the hornet's nest of ambition and intrigue I was going to uncover.

It turns out that about seven years before I arrived, the Finns bought a plot of land as a summer residence in Talbieh, an area about one mile outside the walls of the city. James described it as a place to escape "the miasma" of the city during the greater part of the year. Up until then they used to just set up a tent on a field northwest of Jerusalem and spend some of the hotter days there. James once told me their daughter Constance was born inside that tent the day after Elizabeth had spent a whole afternoon entertaining the pasha's wife and her entourage.

The Finns were the first European family to dare live outside the city walls. The purchase of the Talbieh house was made through James's dragoman Moussa Tannous, a Christian Arab of Egyptian origin, as Europeans are not allowed to own land.

Elizabeth invited me out one afternoon to visit there. It was a sweltering summer day and the relatively cool air of the area was quite a relief. The house itself is a small, square, one-story stone structure, built, of course, by Jewish laborers. The plot around the house is used for growing vegetables, trees and flowers. Near the house and the garden there are seven or eight tents set up amid the rocks, trees and bushes for the workmen to escape the midday sun.

The Finns employ some fifty Jews at this new residence. The more they employ, the more people come looking for work. I noticed a few men sitting under a tree near one of the tents. They seemed weary but happy, much happier than their fellow Jews inside the walls who spend most of their time at endless prayer.

The atmosphere was tranquil. We sat outside drinking lemonade. When Elizabeth told me about her dreams for her and James's projects, her face took on a contented glow.

"For me this work comes from my religious beliefs. I believe the redemption of the Jews is at hand and that they will soon return to their land and to the holy city of Jerusalem, just as you have done, Zara," she told me.

In some ways, I'm envious that she has a mission she can dedicate her life to. There is no doubt that, although the Jewish rabbis are much opposed to James's efforts, this and other projects the Finns are developing are bringing about a tremendous change in attitude among both Christians and Jews. But I still feel uncomfortable with their messianic ambitions. Somehow, I know there will be a price to pay.

A few years after they bought their home in Talbieh, James and Elizabeth purchased another plot of land to the north of the city. It is known to the Arabs as Kerem el-Halil, and to the Jews as Kerem Avraham. But the Finns refer to it as "the Industrial

Plantation." It's an outstanding philanthropic enterprise which has alleviated the distress of hundreds of families.

A few weeks after the Talbieh visit, Elizabeth organized an expedition to the plantation. Since the road from the city to the estate is at times fraught with danger, James sent soldiers with us to guarantee our safety. It was the first time I had ventured out in that direction since I arrived. There was nothing much to see along the way besides the barren, stony landscape one sees everywhere. The only sign of any human habitation was the beginnings of the construction of a huge compound being built by the Russians a few miles outside the city.

After about an hour's walk we arrived at the estate. I was amazed at the size of the place since I knew Elizabeth herself had overseen the construction of the whole complex.

We ate a light meal at a small wooden table in front of the house, and then Elizabeth took me on a tour of the estate. She told me they had bought Kerem Avraham for £250, an enormous sum back in 1852 and even now, and that they were still paying out the cost in payments. The house is quite spacious, but functional, and surrounded by a large plot of land where olives, grapes and vegetables are being cultivated. There is a winepress hewn into the rock, and several water cisterns to provide water for the Jerusalem Jewish population. According to Elizabeth, there are over a hundred laborers working there at any given time, including old men aged seventy and eighty.

After the tour, we walked leisurely back to the walled city. I mused about what might someday occupy this area between Kerem Avraham and the walled city. The Russian complex that was going up was only the beginning. I knew that Conrad had dreams about what could be built in this area and about the large number of Jews that could be brought to live there. We had discussed it many times in our evenings together.

About the Finns' farms near Bethlehem, I heard from other sources. I think Elizabeth found it too difficult to talk about and was not interested in my publishing too many details, either.

I was first informed about them by Bishop Gobat. He once told me about the Meshullams and their farms during one of Elizabeth's soirées. John Meshullam is a British Jew of Greek origin. He converted to Christianity after he met Gobat in Malta several years ago. He arrived in Jerusalem with his son Peter in 1841, five years before the Finns, and opened a hotel, first near the Damascus Gate and later on the Street of the Armenians.

Around 1850, Meshullam, with the aid of Protestant bodies and the Finns, set up a farm in the Arab village of Artas, near Solomon's Pools, just south of Bethlehem.

At first, the enterprise was successful and soon attracted members of an American Protestant sect called the Seventh-Day Adventists. One of the sect's founders was an American woman named Clorinda S. Minor, the wife of a rich Philadelphia businessman. Mrs. Minor was staying at Meshullam's hotel in the Old City. He invited her and her entourage to visit his Artas farm where he and his family were living. She was so impressed by his work that she returned to America and brought over a small group to help attract poor Jews – actual or prospective converts to Christianity – to Meshullam's farm. Eventually she and Meshullam quarreled and Mrs. Minor and her group moved to Jaffa. Elizabeth gained control of the American's property and became Meshullam's partner. According to Gobat, this also resulted in some serious unpleasantness between the Finns and Mrs. Minor, which caused a serious diplomatic confrontation with the United States, a predicament from which they have managed to free themselves only recently.

Relations with Meshullam deteriorated after the Finns purchased the farmstead. Gobat considered this purchase rather rash since the Finns were experiencing severe financial distress at the time and had already been forced to pawn Elizabeth's jewelry to support themselves.

But that was just the beginning. Over the course of time, Elizabeth gained control of various plots in the vicinity of Artas and began to restore them with the aid of Peter Meshullam, whom the Finns have become quite fond of.

The partnership with John Meshullam has now ended, and there have been bitter mutual accusations with regard to financial matters. According to Gobat, these accusations came before James as a judge in such matters. James wrongfully did not disqualify himself from dealing with the matter, and decided, of course, in his wife's favor. Meshullam has now returned to Jerusalem and has become vociferous about the injury caused to him. He blames the Finns for swindling him out of his property.

Things have gotten even more complicated. Last year James gave Peter a position in the consulate, for which he was highly censured by his superiors since many complaints against Peter's conduct had been lodged, including one by the Prince of Wales himself during his visit to Palestine.

I was very torn about writing an article on the Finns. While trying to determine what I in good conscience could include in it and what I might leave out, I decided to pay Elizabeth a visit one afternoon.

When I arrived at her home, I found her in a terrible state. I was not used to seeing her lose her composure. Until now she had told me little about their difficulties, but now she was so distraught she could no longer contain herself. She showed me a letter that James had just received from the British foreign secretary, Lord Russell.

"Oh, Zara, I don't know what to do," she moaned. "We invested all our savings in our projects and James even gave over his salary to cover what we owe. We're penniless! I keep telling myself that God will come to our aid and I'm sure he will but even so, we must make some hard decisions. And what is worse, I feel we have been betrayed by our friends, although I would never tell this to anyone but you. And the most terrible thing is that James may lose his position."

I tried to comfort her but there was not much to say. It's clear they have been reckless in their dealings and entirely too trusting of the people they care for.

I now know that a lot of James's difficulties have to do with his character. I once had an interesting conversation about James with Mary Eliza Rogers, the sister of Edward Rogers, James's associate – fondly known by her friends as Auntie MER. This conversation has cleared up a lot of things for me.

According to Auntie MER, James came from a poor family. He was fortunate enough to be taken under the wing of a British lord, who later became the British foreign secretary. This lord paid for James's education. James later worked as a private tutor in the home of Lord George Aberdeen, another future foreign secretary. It was during his employment there that he began to take an interest in the Jewish religion and to study Hebrew. His strong Protestant beliefs and his interest in the Jews brought him to join the London Jews' Society.

Through his connections, even though he was an unlikely candidate, James was appointed British consul in Palestine. He never overcame his feelings of inferiority with regard to his humble beginnings. On the other hand his appointment to such a powerful post has given him excessive confidence, causing him to behave in an arrogant and superior fashion. That is why, according to Auntie MER, he's often inflexible and willful. Some people blame his behavior on Elizabeth, whom they see as overly ambitious and assertive.

All they say about James may be true but I still believe he has carried out his responsibilities with honor and courage. No other foreign diplomat has done so much to protect and defend the rights of the local population even at the danger of reprimand by his superiors.

I'm going to send the article to you first. Please censor whatever you think is inappropriate as I'm too close to the situation to judge.

Love,
Zara

PART III

Chapter 18

Rebecca Comes Up
with an Idea

Oren and Rebecca had spent the afternoon covering the formerly cream-colored walls of his apartment with a second coat of white paint. His aunt had recently moved into an old-age home and offered him her place in Talpiot – one of the older neighborhoods in the south of the city – which he had gladly accepted.

Most of their free time Oren and Rebecca still spent exclusively with one another, not yet ready to share it with outsiders. They walked around the city, went to movies, shopped on Fridays at the Mahane Yehuda Market. They had no end of topics to talk about but, till now, hadn't really told each other much about their family histories.

After finishing the day's paint job, they both sunk into Aunt Mira's somewhat tattered armchairs and put their feet up on her equally shabby ottoman. They were sharing a meal of yogurt, finely chopped Israeli salad and scrambled eggs. The pleasant weariness they were feeling after the physical exertion and the memories that had come to Oren's mind of his childhood visits to his aunt's home got him talking about his family. "My mother's grandparents were killed in the Holocaust. Her mother was brought to England at the age of six on the *Kindertransport* with my Aunt Mira and she spent her childhood in Manchester." Seeing Rebecca's blank look, he explained. "The *Kindertransport* was an operation to save German Jewish children from the Nazis. My grandmother and my great-aunt were among the thousands of children sent to England by their parents to be taken in by English families. *Safta* came here to live on a kibbutz, where she met my grandfather and where my mother grew up and still lives today.

"I think my grandmother's experience in the war has a lot to do with my attitude to the Jewish religion as well as to my choice of a career. Historical facts are for me far more trustworthy than the ephemeral beliefs of religion. And the kibbutz where I was brought up taught socialist, secular values rather than religious ones."

Rebecca learned that Oren's father was a third-generation Israeli and a well-known poet, although most days he worked in the kibbutz factory. His mother was a literature teacher but was now retired and served as the kibbutz librarian and archivist. From the way Oren talked, it was clear she was the dominant figure in his life.

Oren returned an errant lock of blond hair to its rightful place with a quick flick and continued. "I have two older brothers. One lives on the kibbutz and the other, to my mother's dismay, married a German kibbutz volunteer and now lives with her and my two nephews in Munich. My mother cannot bring herself to travel there to see them, but they visit the kibbutz almost every summer. You really must come down and meet my family."

"I'd love to. But tell me more about you."

"Well, I went to the regional school – sometimes – and then I joined the army and served in a combat unit. At the time, I was very patriotic. I felt I was fighting for my mother's family, who never got the opportunity to protect themselves." Rebecca couldn't imagine such a gentle person killing or even injuring anyone.

"After the army, I moved to Jerusalem. I left behind a childhood girlfriend on the kibbutz. We had moved in different directions and

I couldn't see myself spending the rest of my life with her or in the suffocating kibbutz atmosphere. I studied at Bezalel Art School and since then I've been working at the museum. And that's about it. Quite ordinary, actually."

"For Israel, maybe."

Rebecca then told him a little about her childhood, her parents and her grandmother, and gave him an abridged version of her marriage to Warren. She found it even harder than he did to talk about personal subjects.

To cut the conversation short, she got up and took the dinner dishes into the kitchen. When she came back, she changed the subject. "The exhibit is going quite well, I think. It's almost finished and everyone at the museum seems quite satisfied with it."

She then took a deep breath. "I have a new idea I've been meaning to talk to you about." She paused for a second to see how receptive he was. He seemed to be listening attentively. "You know I've been reading Zara's journals all year."

"Yeah."

"Well, I think her life story could be an exciting subject for an exhibit. What do you think?"

Oren understood immediately that Rebecca's new project was just as much a personal search as a professional one. He thought for a minute or two and then said, "Why don't you do some research into her letters and journals, visit some of the places she mentions in her articles, and come up with a proposal."

"Wow! Great. I will."

"And Rebecca," he added. "Would you like to go to the Reform synagogue near your house on Friday night? You can get an idea of what it's all about."

"OK, I'd like that."

Rebecca's enthusiasm grew over the next few days. The Friday night service at the Reform synagogue was interesting but she found it hard to relate to. Maybe it was because she hadn't grown up with religion at all. Maybe it was because she didn't have a family of her

own yet and belonging to this kind of community meant being involved in more than just religious services. While the chanting went
on she found herself still musing about Zara's visit to the Wall.

By Saturday she was ready to begin her first explorations for
her research. She set off with a guidebook early in the morning from
her home in Baka to the nearby neighborhood of Talbieh, once
the summer home of the Finns. As usual on Shabbat, the streets
were virtually traffic free and all she passed were devout believers
hurrying off to prayers at the nearest synagogue that offered their
particular brand of Judaism.

On her way to Talbieh, she passed through the German Colony,
an upscale neighborhood where she often did her shopping or met
Oren for lunch in one of its many restaurants.

According to her guidebook, the area on which Talbieh was
built had once been a battlefield between the people from the
nearby Arab village of Beit Safafa and the people of Abu Ghosh,
the belligerent Arab village near which Zara's caravan had stopped
on her way to Jerusalem. Beit Safafa was now part of Jerusalem and
Abu Ghosh a large town about ten minutes west of Jerusalem. She
and Oren had recently attended a classical music festival there.

Rebecca walked up to Wingate Square, looking for a building
with the Arabic words *et-talabije* written on it. This, she knew, had
been the Finns' home. She soon found it. There was little difference between it and the other elegant stone buildings on the street.
She stood for a while in front trying to imagine how it must have
looked when it was the only building in the area, surrounded by
cultivated land.

She then continued through the center of town to the Ticho
House, a branch of the Israel Museum where she had recently attended an exhibit on Moses Wilhelm Shapira. This building had
once been his home.

She crossed the Street of the Prophets to Beit Tabor, the home
of Zara's dear friend Conrad Schick and his family, which had been
designed by Schick himself. There she was greeted by a resident of

the Swedish Theological Seminary, the present occupants of the building.

The man was pleased to show her around. He explained that, to this day, the place is considered by the locals as a model of architectural excellence. "We have dozens of visitors coming to see it every year," he said.

He led her to a sunny corner of the building's pleasant courtyard. While they sipped the coffee brought out to them by one of the seminary students, Rebecca told him what she knew about Schick from Zara's journals. The Swede filled in the rest.

"The ties Schick made with the London Jews' Society continued for fifty years. People soon began to recognize his talents and allowed him to indulge his personal interests – the making of models, designing buildings and neighborhoods, and above all, researching Jerusalem and its antiquities.

"These hobbies made him famous. Copies were made of his models and exhibited around the world. Hundreds of his articles and drawings of Jerusalem appeared in international publications. Schick was considered one of the most serious researchers on Jerusalem at the time.

"He also designed some of the important buildings and neighborhoods in the city. One of the first buildings he designed was the Talitakumi, a missionary girls' school in the center of town. Today all that's left of it is a gate. It stands in front of the Hamashbir department store."

"I've seen it a number of times. People use it often as a meeting place."

"Yes, that's right. He is accredited with having planned many of the neighborhoods of modern Jerusalem, like the Orthodox Jewish neighborhood of Mea Shearim, which is not far from here.

"But despite all his important work I understand that Schick remained as modest as he was when he first arrived," the Swede concluded.

Rebecca thanked him for taking the time to talk with her and walked on. She continued to Kerem Avraham, where the Finns had established their plantation. Rebecca's guidebook told her that by 1900 the Finns' house on the plantation had become a soap factory, which was then sold to the British during their rule of the country at a very high price. According to the book, in 1920 the Kerem Avraham neighborhood was founded below the house and it gradually swallowed up the plantations and orchards. Under British rule the house underwent various transformations. First it was a British institute for young offenders, then the property of the British administration, and finally an army headquarters.

Today, it's a religious Jewish girls' school called Beit Bracha, and the neighborhood, usually referred to as Geula, is an Orthodox one – not particularly receptive to sparsely clad females, as Rebecca soon discovered when two outraged religious men in black suits looked away in disgust as she walked down the street. A woman with a scarf on her head shouted "*zona!*" venomously out her window, which Rebecca knew meant "prostitute."

She walked back across town looking for more signs of Zara's world, but didn't recognize any. When she met up with Oren at his apartment later that day she told him about her unpleasant experience in Geula.

"Not all ultra-Orthodox Jews are like that. It's a small group of extremists that make relations so difficult," he explained. "There are also other Orthodox Jews that are less extreme. For example, Hezi and Rahel from the museum are Orthodox and I think you get along with them pretty well, don't you? Maybe we should invite them for dinner on Friday and you could ask them about some of the things that are bothering you."

Then he handed her a book that he thought might help her research. It was an autobiography by the famous Israeli writer Amos Oz called *A Tale of Love and Darkness*. "Oz lived in Geula as a child and writes about the Finn's house in his time. You might enjoy reading it."

Rebecca flipped through the book in the evening and found the section about Oz's impressions of the house when he was a child. He told an amusing anecdote about verbal exchanges between him and his friends and Italian POWs imprisoned in the house at the time. When Oz went back to visit as an adult he described his feelings thus: "I stand at the entrance to Consul Finn's house for a few minutes and gaze at it. The old house has shrunk over the years, as though its head has been pushed down into its shoulders with an axe blow. It has been judaised."

That evening Rebecca put all the material she had collected into a folder, including the notes she had taken on her walk, and sat down to prepare a proposal for the exhibit.

Chapter 19

The Departure of Dear Friends

An excerpt from a letter to Helga, August 1863:

…I knew some day I would be separated from James and Elizabeth, my dear friends and supporters. The truth is I always thought I would be the one to go first. But their term has ended and they have to leave.

Over the years, I have come to depend on them for advice, friendship and a good deal of practical assistance. I could truly say that at this point in my life they are my dearest friends here. In truth, I can't imagine anyone ever taking their place in my heart.

The circumstances under which James has been removed from his position only prove to me what true and loyal friends he and Elizabeth can be. I am not sure that Peter Meshullam was worth their loyalty. I found him extremely arrogant and overbearing. He acted cruelly to the peasants on the farm and dispossessed them of their property. He also caused grave damage to the consulate's relations with the rural population. James chose not to heed the complaints lodged against him and always promoted him as his protégé. Their exceptional fondness for him led them to overlook his shortcomings. Nevertheless,

Peter's violent murder by the Bedouin tribesmen and peasants because of his fraudulent deeds has been a great shock to us all.

The other complaints against James only confirm for me what a determined man he is. It is true that he has a nervous temperament and perhaps has been guilty of putting his trust at times in the wrong persons and distancing himself from those who caution him. But there is no doubt in my mind that he has not participated knowingly in anything fraudulent or criminally improper.

In June, a while after the new consul took on his duties, James and Elizabeth remained to settle their debts. A judge was sent from Britain to assist them. He helped considerably lower the interest charges on James's loans, reducing his debts by half. I must say that Judge Hornby was quite a gentleman and treated the Finns in a forgiving and understanding manner. He, like Auntie MER, blamed James's troubles on his obdurate character. He also blamed Elizabeth for the vast sums she had expended to improve the conditions of the Jews, impoverishing her husband in the process.

I will miss my dearest Elizabeth, whose wisdom and love have helped me through many a troubled and lonely hour. I know she mismanaged her business affairs but I believe her motives were pure. She is a talented woman with amazing courage and strength of character. But most of all she is an outstanding friend.

I am facing quite a personal dilemma as a result of all of this as well. An official at the American Consulate has approached me again, this time to write a report for them about the Artas affair. I have serious reservations about doing this and will have to think it over carefully before I respond.

As always,
Love,
Zara

Chapter 20

A Letter to Helga about a Future Article on the Russian Compound

February 1865

Dear Helga,

I have been thinking about you a lot lately. I follow the news of the war over there and can't imagine what it must be like to have brother fighting against brother, American against American. I hope all is well with you and yours. My boys write that they are fine, safely out of the hostilities. But I worry. Please write and tell me the truth. I know I can rely on you.

I am just about to go off for an interview with the representative of the Russian church here in preparation for an article on the new Russian compound that has been recently completed. It is the Russians' first project outside the city walls, what people are beginning to call the New Jerusalem. Since the end of the Crimean War, the Russians have been trying to create a corner for themselves in the city. Thousands of devout Russian pilgrims make their way here each year at Easter time. They say their numbers reach fourteen thousand. I'm sure you remember my first article about the Ceremony of the Holy Fire.

The Russians have now started a shipping company, which not only brings over pilgrims but also the necessary materials to build their enormous complex. It spreads over eighteen acres and includes a cathedral, a residence for the religious mission, a consulate, a hospital and separate hostels for men and women. It will accommodate over two thousand pilgrims.

Conrad has told me a lot about the site as well. He's terribly interested in it for its archeological significance. He and Edward Robinson, an American professor who calls himself a "biblical geographer," believe that the workers have unintentionally dug up the remains of the third wall that surrounded ancient Jerusalem at the time of Agrippa, the Roman king of Judea. They have also uncovered a large stone pillar they attribute to the time of the Second Temple.

I am often overwhelmed by the immersion of these men and many others who come here to dig into times so distant one cannot even conjure up the thought of them. You cannot lift a rock in this country without coming across some dramatic archeological find. Sometimes I feel that every piece of gravel under my feet is the bones of some ancestor.

I first saw the walls of the Russian Compound begin to go up about five years ago on my walk with Elizabeth to Kerem Avraham, but construction was stopped for a long while due to lack of funds. Rumor has it that someone ran off with a lot of the money. I'll check that out as well during the interview. I hope to send off an article within the month.

By the way, my new contract is again very generous. I'm sure your helpful hand was in it. Again, I thank you. Now that my column carries a byline I get lots of interesting mail, especially from people planning to visit here, and their numbers are growing.

Take care of yourself and answer soon.

Your dearest friend,

Zara

Chapter 21

Zara Disappears

May 4, 1865

Dear Reverend Schick,

Forgive me for being so bold as to write to you without any reference from a mutual acquaintance, but I don't know where else to turn. I am a close friend of Zara Rubens from New York and I'm aware of your friendship with her over the years. She has always talked about you as a kind, intelligent man who is deeply involved in the life of the city and I thought you might be able to assist me.

The last time I heard from Zara was over three months ago when she wrote she intended to forward an article she was writing on the Russian Compound. The editors at the New York Times have informed me that, although she had committed to sending it three months ago, they have received nothing. They sent her several letters and of late two or three telegraphs to the new telegraph station in Jaffa. There has been no reply to any of their missives, nor to any of mine nor those of her sons. This is untypical of her and we are very worried.

I would be grateful if you could shed any light on this mystery or refer me to someone who can. Just so you should know I'm sending copies of all my letters to Palestine regarding Zara to the American government here in New York and keeping one for myself.

Yours very gratefully,
Helga Ehrlich

Jerusalem, 1 June, 1865

Dear Mrs. Ehrlich,

    I am familiar with your name as Zara has mentioned you several times in our conversations. Since I have been much occupied in the last few months the distance between my meetings with Zara was farther apart. So I am sorry to say I was not aware of her disappearing. I have told the American and British officials about this and they are doing as well as they can to discover her. They did not know that she was working on an article about the Russian Compound. By the grace of God, this will allow them to find her more quickly.

    I assure you that for me Zara is also a dear friend and I will direct all my attentions to help discover her location.

    Yours very truly,
    Conrad Schick

June 25, 1865

Dear Reverend Schick,

    I'm sorry to bother you again but I cannot get Zara out of my mind. I'm beginning to fear the worst. I know I won't be of much help but I feel it is necessary for me to make my way over to your city in person to do what I can to move the investigations along.

    Unless I receive any positive news from you in the near future, I will book my passage over. The one good thing will be that perhaps I will have the opportunity to make the acquaintance on this occasion of you and your family.

    Sincerely,
    Helga Ehrlich

PART IV

Chapter 22

Rebecca at the Russian Compound

Rebecca continued to read Zara's journals and prepare for the exhibit. One evening she and Oren were sitting in his living room. Oren was at the desk working on some research for the museum and Rebecca decided to get on with her project. She brought the box of journals she was presently working her way through into the room, made herself a cup of coffee and sat down to read, a yellow legal pad at her side. She had recently finished reading the journal that ended in December 1864 so she looked in the box for the next volume. It wasn't there. She went to look for it in Oren's storeroom where she was keeping the rest of the boxes but it wasn't there either. She could only find some letters from that time. She read them as she walked back into the apartment.

"I'm missing a journal covering six months of Zara's life," she said to Oren.

"How could that be? Did you check all the boxes?"

"Yeah, I did."

"Maybe it got lost somewhere along the way. It's been a hundred and fifty years, you know. It's surprising you have so many of them. Or maybe she just stopped writing for a while."

"She didn't always write a lot but she made sure to write a few lines each week just to remind herself of what had happened. But look at these letters between Helga and Conrad Schick," she said, passing them to Oren. "I think something bad happened to her. It looks like it had to do with her article on the Russian Compound."

"Check it out," Oren suggested after reading them.

"I intend to."

Rebecca decided to talk to someone at the Russian mission. When she called there the next day, a solemn gentleman with a strong Russian accent and broken English answered. She explained that she was doing research on a woman by the name of Zara Rubens for the Israel Museum. The mention of the museum got her an appointment with an official there for the following afternoon.

She was uneasy all the next morning, as if something terrible were going to happen to her when she entered the compound. On the bus to town, she reread Helga's and Conrad's letters, looking for clues. Helga seemed very anxious in her letter, not at all in keeping with her character. Rebecca had by now come to know Zara and her acquaintances as well as her own friends.

She reached town about fifteen minutes before her appointment and walked slowly down Jaffa Road until she got to the corner nearest the compound. She climbed the hill leading up to the Russian Orthodox Church. On her left was the police station and on her right the court buildings. She turned right at the church, right again, and found the mission at the rear, as she had been told she would. She knew from her reading that all the buildings in this area had once belonged to the Russians but that the area of the compound left in Russian hands today had been much reduced.

She rang the bell and waited nervously. It was soon opened by a Russian Orthodox priest, who turned out to be the official Rebecca was meant to meet. Her host was dressed in the flowing black robes of the Russian Orthodox Church with a huge, three-barred cross hanging from his neck. His shoulder-length hair had been freshly washed and neatly arranged in the style of what Rebecca's grandmother used to call a pageboy hairdo. His skin was white and flawless and his deep blue eyes seemed compassionate, which calmed Rebecca somewhat.

With the aid of an interpreter, he guided her around the quarters. They were tastefully decorated with restored nineteenth-century furniture, plush carpets and burgundy velvet curtains. The official then invited her to tea in the small courtyard of the mission and shared with her some of his reasons for coming to the country and his feelings about being there. His monologue seemed rehearsed, as if he had repeated it several times before to other visitors. Nevertheless, it helped Rebecca feel more at ease.

They then went inside. He led her to a small room at the back of the mission and sat down behind a large mahogany desk. He gestured for her to sit across from him. She decided not to take out her tape recorder as she had planned, so as not to put him off.

"Since our conversation on the phone I have taken the opportunity to look into the matter you are interested in," he explained through his interpreter. He then paused for a long minute, examining her carefully to see if she was really what she claimed to be. There was a large, alluring file on his desk and Rebecca was impatient to get her hands on it.

In an effort to allay any fears he might have, she pulled her museum card out of her bag. He looked at the card closely, checking to see if the young woman in front of him matched the image in the photograph. He decided it was safe to continue.

"When I first arrived here I did a lot of research into the history of this place. The building once housed an enormous library, although much of it was transferred elsewhere many years ago. In 1964, an agreement was made with the Israeli government and the whole compound was bought from the Russian Church except for these rooms," he said, indicating the rooms they had passed through earlier. "The agreement came to be known as the Orange Deal because it involved the export of Israeli citrus to the Soviet Union in partial exchange for the land and the building." He again

paused, slowly opening the file in front of him. Rebecca was beginning to feel hopeful.

"Many papers were stored in the basement rooms," he explained. "I went down every so often to put them in order. When I
heard you were interested in Zara Rubens, I remembered the name
and after some hunting around was able to put my hands on this."
He pointed to the file and lifted a journal from it for her to see,
which till now had lain hidden inside the file.

Rebecca recognized one of her aunt's now familiar brown-and-
yellow, leather-bound journals. She clutched at her bag to control
her excitement.

"I am ashamed to tell you that I have discovered that, due to
some terrible misunderstanding, this woman, Zara Rubens, was imprisoned in our women's hostel across the road for several months.
I have no idea what happened to her after that."

He indicated a large building a few hundred meters away on
the far side of a municipal parking lot. "The Museum of Jewish
Underground Prisoners is located there today," he explained.

"I believe this is the journal she kept during her imprisonment," he said, lifting it again, enticingly, "which I must tell you
I have taken the liberty to read. I think you will find it extremely
interesting. For us it is a black spot in our history and one best
forgotten. I hope you will respect our wishes."

Rebecca was speechless. How could it be that such a treasure
had been sitting there just waiting for someone to discover it all
these years? Hadn't anyone been curious about this period in Zara's
life before? Why hadn't Zara gone back to get it?

It looked like the church official was going to turn over the
file and journal to her without any problem. There was no doubt
that the period during which anyone could be brought to trial for
crimes committed at the time had long passed.

He withdrew a large manila envelope from the desk and put the
file and the journal inside it. He then passed it over to Rebecca.

She thanked him, perhaps too profusely, for his assistance. Only after the envelope was safely in her possession did she explain to him that Zara was her relative and that she was planning on doing an exhibit at the Israel Museum on Zara's life in Palestine based on her journals and letters.

The official seemed uncomfortable with this information but nevertheless satisfied with his decision.

"I will, of course, be very careful to present this episode in her life in a fair and sympathetic fashion," Rebecca added reassuringly. "As a man with a passion for history you can imagine how exciting it is to discover such an interesting member of one's own family." Rebecca stopped there, not wanting to do anything to make him change his mind.

She took her leave as soon as she could, stuffing the envelope into her large bag on the way out. Outside the mission, she considered going across the road to visit the hostel in which her great-great-aunt had been incarcerated so many years before but she was too curious to read the journal. The visit could wait for another day.

When she got home, she made herself a sandwich, got comfortable on the living room sofa and took out the journal, handling it with great care. It had certainly seen a lot of wear and tear. She made a mental note to ask the museum restorers to work their magic on it. She had also brought up the next journal from the basement, which she soon discovered completed the story of Zara's imprisonment.

Chapter 23

Zara's Story

February 12, 1865

I must record everything that happens to me here. I must reproduce events as faithfully as I can. It may be the only way family and friends will ever know what happened to me. All I can hope is that someone will someday come upon my journal and pass it on. If my stay here is long, I will slowly lose touch with reality. I must discipline myself to stick to my task. Let me first record what has happened in the past twenty-four hours.

The church spokesman who greeted me upon my arrival at the compound overwhelmed me with his entrance into the room. Dressed in the typical Russian, black-hooded clerical garment, he swept down upon me with the energy of a hawk about to attack. The enormous golden cross hanging from his neck seemed to me like the flesh of some recently slaughtered prey. His pitch-black hair and long nails were immaculately groomed. This was a man who had never seen a day's physical labor in his life. A set of iron keys hung from a cord around his waist.

As polished as his appearance was, his speech was even more so. He spoke slowly and clearly, weighing every word and doing his best to impose his authority on me. His nervous interpreter, fearing for his life – probably quite rightly so – translated his words with painful exactitude.

The interview began normally enough. I think I've honed my interviewing skills over the years sufficiently to be able to extract the most intimate and exact details from my subjects in the shortest amount of time.

I managed to get the basic information out of him quite quickly. But the spokesman skillfully skirted more delicate issues. Reference, for example, to the bitter rivalry between the Russian, German and Anglican churches for the hearts of the natives and for political control in the area he just ignored or redirected into channels he chose to elaborate on.

He talked a lot about the faith and sincerity of the pilgrims coming to the new compound, how their numbers were increasing by the thousands yearly, and how Russian influence in the Holy Land was growing enormously. He then went on to describe the architecture of the various buildings, explaining that some were of Renaissance style and that some had a much stronger Byzantine influence. He also described the plans of the Russian Church to expand the complex even further.

All was proceeding quite amicably and then I made my mistake. I don't know why I let myself in for these things. Why couldn't I just mind my own business? It was probably my overdeveloped sense of justice, which has often caused me difficulties. But I did it. And for that, I am now suffering.

At first, I innocently let drop a question about why the construction had been stopped for a period of time just after building had begun. The official provided me with the stock reply that unavoidable political and bureaucratic constraints had forced them to look for alternate forms of financing. And then I put my foot into it. I remember my exact words.

"There have been stories that some church official absconded with the money, millions of rubles I understand. Is there any truth in that?"

I expected him to evade the subject as he had done others but instead he promptly dropped his diplomatic façade as if he were shedding his winter feathers and lowered his voice considerably. "Where did you hear that?" he whispered, leaning ominously forwards, coming in for the kill. The cross dangling from his neck almost touched my face.

I told him they were just rumors. I can't even recall how I heard of the theft, although if I could I would not implicate my sources. Little did I know how much I had implicated myself.

"The rumors you have heard are completely false and I suggest you stop spreading them as they are slanderous and can cause you a lot of difficulties," was his restrained reply. The message was clear even before the translator managed to blurt it out.

For some reason I considered his aggressiveness a challenge and I foolishly continued to defy him. I began to ask not very diplomatic questions about the political rivalry between the Russians and the other European powers in the city. From then on, the official responded to my questions in monosyllables and then suddenly he stood up and said, "Perhaps you would like to have a tour of the compound."

I immediately agreed as I realized it was time to put an end to this painful situation, and we set off to visit the newly completed buildings. He left the women's residence for last. When we arrived at this huge, E-shaped, monastic building he directed me towards one of the many rooms meant to serve as quarters for female pilgrims. There was not much to see – a mattress on the floor, a wooden chair, a huge Russian cross on the wall, and a small kerosene lamp next to a Bible on a tiny bedside table. I took a quick glance around and turned to walk out again when suddenly the door was slammed shut in my face and locked. I protested loudly but the spokesman made no response. I could hear his officious footsteps clicking away down the hall at a rapid pace.

It took me a while to comprehend what was happening to me, to make the connection between the aborted interview and my present situation. After a while, it began to sink in. I looked around and discovered there were iron bars on the window, their primary purpose presumably to provide protection from thieves. I was locked in, a prisoner of my own brazenness.

As the hours passed, I began to evaluate my situation. What is going to become of me? People in this part of the world deal with such issues in a very definite fashion. My only hope is that someone will discover I'm missing and come looking for me. Since the Finns left, there is only one person I'm in daily contact with these days and that's Carrie. Unfortunately, Carrie went off to England a couple of days ago to visit her daughter and will probably be away for months. If Aya were still working for me, I could rely on her to inform someone at the consulate. It's a shame I had to let her go, but I just could no longer afford her services. As for Conrad, he has become too busy with other matters to notice my absence, although our improbable friendship has deepened over the years. Even if my sons or Helga or the Times begin to wonder about my whereabouts it will be months before they take any action. And God knows what will happen to me by then. I'm in deep trouble.

Perhaps this is just a temporary misunderstanding and I'll soon be released once they realize they're dealing with an American citizen and that such behavior is unacceptable in civilized society. But it's possible I'll be imprisoned indefinitely – or worse.

I lay down on the mattress and did my best to rest, which of course was a waste of time. After what seemed like hours, I heard someone unlocking the door. I felt relieved until I saw the spokesman had returned with someone even more officious looking than himself. While the spokesman reminded me of a hawk, this one was more like a vulture. Dressed in the same black robes, his long locks were of a pale red color, clean, and well coiffed. His piercing black eyes only added to his commanding appearance. He had come not to listen but to talk. He needed no interpreter. He spoke perfect English, although strongly accented, making it even more menacing.

"Madam, it is my duty to inform you that the head of the Russian Church Mission has decided you must stay incarcerated here until you can inform us who has been spreading these false rumors about our venerable mission. There are other issues as well that we must discuss with you. We assure you that although we shall respect the fact that you are a reputable woman we will take whatever measures we find necessary to obtain this information from you."

I wanted to reply but the words stuck in my throat. He didn't wait long enough for me to get them out. After a few seconds he turned around swiftly, his robe billowing around him, and exited the room. Again, I heard the heavy click of the door being locked.

Wednesday evening, February 13

The sun is setting. I can hear the bells from Christ Church all the way to my cell.

I tossed and turned last night trying to find some solution to my predicament. And when I did finally fall asleep, I was woken soon after by the chirping of the birds in the courtyard. Under different circumstances, this could be a place for a pleasant retreat.

About an hour later, the key turned in the door again. I cowered in the corner expecting the worst. Instead, a black-sleeved hand gently pushed a tray into the room with a simple breakfast on it of white cheese, dark bread, cracked green olives and a cup of thick black Turkish coffee. It then withdrew and the door was again locked. As soon as I heard the footsteps receding down the hall, I went straight for the coffee and drank it up thirstily. I thought back to the first cup of this coffee I had tasted on my journey up to Jerusalem with Dimitri so long ago. And of course, that brought to mind the old Jew who died on that journey. For some reason he has often entered my thoughts during my life in this country.

The day has passed uneventfully. The hand came through later to remove the tray and replace it with a basin of water covered with a towel along with a few pieces of coarse paper. I understood I was first to use the basin for washing and then for relieving myself. I found this extremely demeaning, but there's nothing I can do. I have learned to live with some very primitive conditions during my life here and this is just another thing I'll have to adjust to.

The boredom of the day has been relieved only by the same anonymous hand removing the basin a few hours later and at noon returning with another modest meal. This time the offering included pita bread, a small piece of overcooked chicken and rice. He also passed through a black dress for me to change into. I'm glad to have something else to wear, although it makes me look rather nun-like.

A few female pilgrims are coming and going outside my door speaking their throaty language in reverential whispers. I hear a few words of their conversation but cannot piece them together. It's not the time of the pilgrimages but some Christians seem to have stayed on. I think about calling out to them but I know it's not wise.

Tuesday

I can't believe I've been here a week now. No one has come to either console or threaten me. I suppose their plan is to wear me down with solitude until I can no longer cope with the lack of human contact and will tell them what they want to know.

Over the days, the hand that slips me my meals has taken on a new meaning for me. It is a kind presence, a caring soul. I find myself longing to follow the arm along and meet the full figure at the end.

Any sense of urgency I had to escape has disappeared. I spend my days with my thoughts. Sometimes I think about what might become of me and I'm overcome with a feeling of panic. But then I convince myself there is no purpose in this and I let my mind wander wherever it chooses.

Often I go back over what I've experienced in the past nine years. For the thousandth time I try to uncover somewhere in the depths of my soul why I chose to come here at all.

What possessed me? What was I searching for? I have no real answers, although I do know that I wouldn't have missed the experiences I've had and the people I've met for the world. America is an exciting place, although these years life there must be precarious as well, with the Civil War and all. But America is not my home. It's not where I belong.

Yet what makes this forsaken piece of desert a more attractive abode for me I cannot say, even as a Jew. There is no doubt that the biblical stories my grandmother read to me as a child made an impression, and when I go to a place that has biblical significance I do feel a connection. Conrad knows his Bible and he has been a great teacher in this area. But my Jewishness is very changeable. It's more a product of my state of mind than of any external influence. It alters with my mood, my situation in life, my surroundings.

But there is more to my tie to this place than that. If I believed in reincarnation, I would say I had lived here in a previous life. But, of course, that is ridiculous. This is how my thoughts always end up, at a conclusion unacceptable to my rational mind. And so I leave them again.

The nights are very cold. Yesterday, the Hand passed me a gray shawl through the door with my evening meal. It has a musky smell as if it had been in storage a long time, awaiting my arrival. I wrap myself in it tightly. It feels like the Hand that gave it to me was enfolding me to give me not only warmth but comfort as well.

Wednesday

The official arrived today. He questioned me again. This time I managed to say that I had no answers to give him. He left abruptly without responding. I am terrified. My greatest fear is torture of some kind, which I know I could not endure for long. I'm too old for this. Oh, when will someone come and get me out of here!

March

I heard the Sunday church bells ringing this morning. They help me keep track of the days. The nights are so long, I feel they are never-ending. I have developed a chill which I hope won't turn into anything worse. Who knows? I may die from the cold without anyone knowing. The Hand has again taken pity on me and added a thick chicken broth to my evening meal, which warms me for a while before I face the cold nights. Today the Hand also passed me a couple of extra coarse, gray woolen blankets. I shiver under them till I drift off for a few hours in the middle of the night.

I've been thinking a lot about my boys these days. What must they feel about their mother? I am so ashamed to have deserted them. They expected me to stay home and be a real grandmother to their children, to help them with motherly advice, to fill my place in the passage of the generations. I deserve to be left alone here to die like this. I've brought it upon myself.

Tuesday – I think

I haven't gotten out of bed for days. Yesterday I crawled towards the door to take a little nourishment and relieve myself but that was all I could manage. I think I'm becoming delirious. Last night I dreamt I was a child again in Russia.

It is a cold, wintry day in the shtetl. I am walking through a morass of mud on the way to my teacher's house for lessons. Walking beside me is Alex. We are holding hands. We reach the teacher's house and the teacher asks what Alex is doing there. "He is my husband," I answer. The teacher accepts that explanation with equanimity and lets us into the lesson. Then this dream is cut short by another. I dream that a figure in a black cloak comes into the room to bring me some food and put a basin down on my bedside table. At times, I see him as the angel of death, at times the angel of mercy. But there it is! The basin is on my bed table. Did I put it there? I don't know.

Date: ?

I am beginning to come back to myself. I have so much to write
about. I don't know where to start. From what I understand, my
fever became very high and I was close to death. The figure in
black is not a hallucination but the angel that has been taking
care of my needs. My condition was so critical that he had to
care for me twenty-four hours a day. He put compresses on
my head, fed me when I would eat, gave me natural herbs
that helped bring down the fever. He also held my hand and
whispered comforting words to me as I tossed and turned.
There was something familiar about this figure. He did his best
not to show me his face, yet I felt a closeness towards him. I
was too weak to make an effort to sit up. Somewhere in my
delirium, I assumed one of my friends or family had come to
take care of me. I didn't have the strength to be curious about
who this person might be and how he had gotten here.

Date: ?

After I don't know how many weeks, my strength has begun to
return and when the figure in black arrived yesterday with my
evening meal, I was sitting up. He was taken aback and drew
the head covering closer in front of his face before he lay the
tray down at my bedside. He was about to withdraw when I
begged him to stay. I tried to thank him for all he had done for
me.

"You have saved my life," I said.

"I no speak English," he answered with a strong Russian
accent.

My heart fell. If he didn't speak English, then he was not
someone I knew. So who was he? "I speak a little Russian,"
I offered. "I was born there. We could talk." He mumbled
something incomprehensible and disappeared out the door,
locking it quickly before hurrying down the hall.

I impatiently awaited his arrival this morning. I had to
talk to this man. I had to find out who he was and what he

knew about my situation. But when the door opened only the Hand came through, as it had before I fell ill. I was terribly disappointed. At lunchtime, I tried to speak to him in Russian when he brought my meal, but he quickly closed the door again. This evening I waited by the door. When I heard him coming, I tensed myself. He put his hand through the doorway and I grabbed it, pulling him into the room.

I don't know where I got the strength, to say nothing of the courage, to do such a thing. He was so shocked that he came in and stood in front of me. His cowl had fallen to his shoulders and he stood there bareheaded and ill at ease. I looked closely at his face. It was the first human face I had seen in months. His skin was deeply lined and his shoulder-length hair was brown, stringy and thinning at the top. There was something unbelievably familiar about him.

"Please come and sit by me for a few minutes," I said in Russian.

He looked at me cautiously. "I cannot to do that. I will get into trouble if I do," he answered.

"Just for a moment," I begged.

He softened and sat down on the chair while I sat on the mattress. "I don't know how to thank you for being so kind to me. I wish I could repay you in some way," I said to him in Russian.

"There is no need. Anyone would have done the same thing," he answered, his eyes boring into the ground.

"Well, in this country that does not seem to be necessarily true. In any case, I thank you with all my heart. Please, tell me your name so I will know to whom I owe my life."

He looked into my eyes, as if expecting a sign of recognition, before he said quietly, "My name is Alex." He then stood up and rushed out of the room.

I am still in shock. Did he say Alex? I keep asking myself. I must still be hallucinating. That cannot be his name. Even if it is, there are millions of Alexes in Russia. It doesn't mean a thing.

But how many are there in Jerusalem? But that's absurd. The Alex I know cannot be here. And, if he is, what is he doing in the Russian Compound? And of all things watching over me? It has to be a coincidence.

Sunday

The church bells woke me again this morning. All day I've been sitting here going over in my mind what happened yesterday. I conjure up the face that emerged from the cowl. I try to decide if this Alex is really my Alex. And if he is, why does he hold back? Why doesn't he talk to me? Perhaps he doesn't recognize me. Perhaps he's forgotten me.

The evening is coming on but still the only contact I've had with him is to see his hand sliding through the door to serve my needs. I look carefully at it each time it comes through. But I don't really remember what Alex's hands were like and even if I did, they have aged, as he and I both have.

I must just be patient. Something will happen.

Monday

Well, what I wrote last night was prophetic. Just before I was drifting off to sleep, I heard the door unlock and in walked Alex. He held his finger to his lips warning me to keep quiet, sat down in the chair beside my bed and began to talk. I must record our conversation word for word. I don't want to ever forget it.

"I think, Zara, you have guessed that it is I, the Alex you knew so many years ago in Russia. I saw them taking you here and volunteered to take care of you, hoping I could in some way make your imprisonment here less painful."

As he talked, I began to recognize the familiar gestures, the halting way in which he spoke. "But why didn't you make yourself known to me sooner?" I asked with almost a whimper in my voice.

"I was afraid you wouldn't remember me, or worse,

wouldn't want to acknowledge our connection."

"Oh, but Alex, you have been in my mind and heart all these many years. How could you believe I wouldn't remember you?"

"I am so moved to hear that, Zara. I've thought of you as well. But I heard you went to America and were married there with a family, so I made no effort to contact you. But how did you end up here, and alone?"

I told him the story of how I was widowed and of my coming to Jerusalem, again stumbling over the explanations for why. I explained that I have been writing a column for a well-known New York newspaper and how I had been planning to do an article on the Russian Compound and stuck my nose in too far.

"But tell me about your life. What has happened to you? What are you doing here in Jerusalem?" I asked.

"I came as a pilgrim, looking for some kind of religious enlightenment and decided to stay. I married an Arab woman."

"So you are married. Do you have any children?"

"We have seven. We lost another five along the way. This is no country for bringing up children."

"I also have two grown boys with children of their own. But I'm a terrible mother and grandmother because when my husband died I soon deserted them all and came here." I could see he was anxious to leave but I couldn't stop talking. "Someone told me you had visited Jerusalem and you were always in the back of my mind though I never dared to search you out. I didn't really believe you were still here."

"Zara, listen to me," he interrupted. "I can't stay much longer. We must do something to get you out of here. They could leave you to die here if we don't."

"I have a dear friend. His name is Conrad Schick –"

"Oh, yes. I have met him. The German reverend. He was around here a lot when they were building the compound."

I tore a piece of paper from my journal and wrote a note to

Conrad along with his address.

"Please go to him. He'll help me. I'm sure," I said, handing him the piece of paper.

"I will. And now I must leave. I'll be back as soon as I can to tell you what he says."

"Thank you, Alex. I hope we'll one day have time to talk under more normal circumstances."

"I, too. Good night, Zara."

"Good night, Alex," I answered, hardly believing this conversation had actually taken place.

I still have my doubts.

Tuesday, late afternoon

This day has been one of the longest in my life. A different hand has served me today, that of a woman. Perhaps it was Alex's wife. Perhaps he's been found out and sent away. But I try to take his absence as a good sign, a sign that he's off in search of Conrad. I'm sure he'll be back tonight.

Wednesday

Not only did Alex arrive last night but Conrad was also with him, disguised in a monk's robe. I was so glad to see him I burst into tears. He's such a sweet, gentle man.

Conrad explained that he didn't think it would be of any use to talk to the Russian representative. The Russians are extremely mistrustful these days, especially towards anyone connected to the English and the Germans, and Conrad has ties to both of them. When he saw my disheartened look, he quickly added, "But I do know a way to get you out of here."

He went on to explain. He said that when they built this compound he had been at the site almost every day looking for archeological finds. He saw that when they were laying the foundations they had also put in some underground tunnels, and he has the plans for the compound, which include those tunnels. One of the tunnels comes up in the women's hostel, so he is arranging for a few of his students to come here tomorrow night and take me out through that tunnel.

He explained the plan to me. Alex will arrive at exactly one in the morning to unlock the door. He'll then disappear so that he in no way will be associated with the escape. That is very important. We must be very careful not to implicate him – he could die for this. He emphasized that my life is also in grave danger. But he added that if I remained here, I may spend the rest of my days in this room. He didn't have to tell me this. I was well aware of that possibility and was ready to take the risk of leaving.

I'm naturally feeling very anxious, but I know Conrad is right and that I don't have much choice in the matter. At the same time, though, I feel an exhilarating sense of adventure after having been locked up here for so many months.

Chapter 24

Conrad Prepares to Free Zara

An excerpt from a letter to Elizabeth Finn:

…I received your letter about Zara yesterday. I know about the matter. Our dear friend has made a diplomatic faux pas and is in trouble with the Russians.

I can tell you about the incident from my point of view. One night I was working at home on my models and there was a knock on the door. When I opened it, a workman from the Russian Compound who I saw there on my recent visits was standing in front of me. He looked very worried. I immediately understood he brought me information about Zara and let him in.

He spoke to me in broken Arabic. He told me the story of Zara's imprisonment and handed me a note from her. He said she was in bad physical condition and that she must be released soon.

I thanked him for coming, which I'm sure had put him in much danger. I told him not to worry, and said I would get back to him as soon as I could.

I began to think about my alternatives. I know the Russian clergy at the compound well. They are very defensive and will not at all appreciate a German interfering in their affairs. After a sleepless night, I came up with a plan to free Zara.

I spent the day making arrangements. I commandeered two of my most trusted students. We studied the maps I made of the compound and planned in detail where we would enter and how we would get Zara out. I instructed my students to collect the necessary equipment, some dark clothing, a few kerosene lamps and a black cloak for Zara. I then got Dimitri, your former dragoman, to be our protector. This mission was no simple task. We could all be murdered and no one would know for months.

I then visited our old friend Bishop Gobat. I told him the whole story and asked him if I could bring Zara there when we got her out. Gobat knows Zara and likes her very much. He immediately agreed to give her protection. He said he would tell his students to keep her presence a secret.

I had one more task. I paid a visit to a Turkish clerk I had dealings with in the past. I gave him a pile of bills and asked him to pay each of the guards on duty at Jaffa Gate that night a generous baksheesh so we could enter the city. The last thing we needed would be problems with the Turks for being illegally abroad at night....

Chapter 25

Zara Describes Her Escape

A room in Gobat's school, July 1865
I have been here for three weeks now. Dear, kind Bishop
Gobat and his wife have been very hospitable and given me
a comfortable room with a view of the Hinnon Valley. After I
bathed and rested for a few hours, I asked about Alex. I was
told he was continuing to work as usual so as not to cast any
suspicion on himself.

Now that I have some time to think again, I must record the
experience of that fearsome night. What I write now of course
can never be published, as I would endanger too many people –
which I know I have done already, in any case.

There was very little I had to do to prepare, as everything
was being done for me. I very carefully hid my journal under a
stone in the floor just in case we should be waylaid. I stamped
down the stone and covered it up with dirt to make it look as
if it had not been touched. It must not be discovered. I hope
that someday I will return to recover it. When Alex arrived that
night, I was ready. He unlocked the door for the last time and
silently motioned to me that it was time to leave. He wished me
luck in a whisper and ran off.

I walked outside and saw Conrad waiting with a young
man beside him, along with, of all people, Dimitri, my first
guide in the Holy Land, with his pistol stuck boldly into the
waistband of his wide pants. I don't know whether it was the
tension or the sight of an old, familiar face or both, but tears
began to roll down my cheeks again.

Conrad threw a black cloak around my shoulders and as he lifted the hood to cover my head, his hand brushed against my arm. A shiver ran down my spine. It might have been from the cold or from fear, but most of all I think it was from the human touch that I'd been deprived of for so long.

We began to cross the courtyard slowly so as to arouse less suspicion if someone should see us. Suddenly, halfway across, Conrad held out a hand to restrain me. I followed the direction of his look and saw a frightened nun on the far side of the courtyard, standing frozen, like a cornered animal. She had probably gotten up to relieve herself and been on the way back to her room when she saw us. Conrad raised a finger to his lips imploring her to keep our secret. We held our breath. She stood still for a second and then rushed off into her room, locking it quickly from the inside.

As we continued across the courtyard, I could hear wild dogs howling off in the distance and an owl on a not-too-distant perch heralding our arrival into the night. We stopped at a room diagonally across the courtyard. Conrad let us in and I recognized one of his favorite students standing over a dark, cavernous hole at the back of the room, his face lit up eerily from below by a kerosene lamp. Beside the hole lay a heavy boulder of Jerusalem stone, which clearly had been covering it until recently.

The first student took the lamp from his friend and crawled inside. Conrad removed my cloak and handed it the student beside him, who inserted it into a small pack on his back. Conrad climbed in and beckoned me to follow. I approached the hole. Under the light of the lamp I could see that there was a rope ladder with about ten rungs attached to the inside of the opening, which led down to an extremely narrow tunnel.

There was no time to hesitate, even though under normal circumstances I would never have agreed to enter such a narrow underground passage. But I did. After I had gone down a few steps, Dimitri followed me. Suddenly a cascade of dirt fell onto my head. I panicked, sure I was going to be buried alive. Dimitri was about to fall on top of me. He was not a heavy man and the ladder was quite new but nevertheless the second rung had suddenly given way under his weight. He nimbly managed, however, to somehow reach down to the more solid fourth rung just above my head and keep from falling all the way down.

I could not move from fear. Conrad reached up and touched my hand lightly. The warmth of his hand brought me back to myself. I soon reached the ground and entered the tunnel behind Conrad. As we passed through the damp passageway, I began to feel as if I were going back in time and that at the end of the tunnel I would come back out into a period far back in history. I imagined us arriving on the Temple Mount, at the time of the Second Temple.

It seemed we walked through the tunnel for hours, although it couldn't have been more than ten minutes. When we finally reached the end, a third young man was waiting and helped each of us to come out onto solid ground. Conrad's student returned the black cloak to me, which I threw over my shoulders and head. I looked around and, as surprising as it seemed to me at the time, we were not somewhere back in the time of the Second Temple but in the present, in the deserted area between the compound and the walled city.

We started running towards the city. The guards at the gate raised their weapons threateningly upon the arrival of this ominous-looking band, but Conrad waved to draw attention to himself. The guards recognized him and let us through. We then proceeded to the school. I am to stay hidden here until Conrad can determine the Russian reaction to my escape.

Chapter 26

Zara Visits Alex

Gobat's school, August 1865

Conrad has been called into the Russian Compound. They
somehow have discovered his part in my escape. Perhaps the
nun told him, perhaps the soldiers at the gate. He explained to
the official that there had been a terrible mistake and that I had
no real knowledge about any wrongdoings with regard to the
church funds. He also reassured them I would take no further
action in the matter and that there was nothing for them to fear.
He apologized for securing my release without their permission
and hoped it would not affect the cordial relations that had
existed between him and the Russian Church till now.

To compensate the church for the embarrassment, he
offered them as a present a detailed model of the compound,
which he had been working on over the past few months.
Conrad's models were so exact and professionally done that
the Russians were very pleased to be given such a valuable gift.
They finally agreed that no repercussions would result from
my deed, but requested that I not publicly discuss any matter
connected to the affair. In any case, I had no intention of doing
so. Conrad warned me, in his fatherly fashion, to be extremely
discreet for a while. The truth was I planned to just rest for the
next few months and get back my strength.

About a month after my arrival here and after Conrad
assured him it was safe to wander around at large, Alex arrived
at the school to invite me to visit him and his family. I gladly
accepted although I was quite anxious about meeting his wife,

143

especially since we would have no common language. All I
knew were the few words in Arabic I had picked up from Aya,
and they mostly related to domestic matters.

I met him the next day at Jaffa Gate. He had brought a
small cart to transport us. His village was about a half hour's
ride away. He said he hoped I would not be too uncomfortable.
I told him I had become quite used to discomfort in the past
while.

Within half an hour, as he promised, we arrived at the
village. It was built up a hill and we had to climb a number of
steps to reach his home. The villagers peered out of their doors
and some children stood outside staring unabashedly at this
foreign woman in their midst. Although they looked quite poor,
they had a sureness in their eyes of who and what they were.
Alex stopped at a small house halfway up the hill.

"This is my home. Welcome," he said. The last word he
said in Arabic, *Marhaba*.

The both of us had to bow our heads to get through the
entrance. Sitting in a circle on a straw mat and leaning on
several cushions were two young men, one of whom looked
very much like Alex, and two small children who had obviously
been warned to be on their best behavior. In the middle of
the room was a large silver tray filled with a variety of Middle
Eastern salads. A middle-aged woman and two teenagers were
standing behind the men and younger children, clearly waiting
to begin serving the rest of the food.

Alex first introduced me to his eldest son, Ahmed, and
his son-in-law, Jamal, and only then to his wife, Yasmin, his
daughter Su'ad, and his daughter-in-law Samira, as well as his
grandchildren. His wife blushed self-consciously. The situation
made her as uncomfortable as it did me. But she smiled as
best she could and pointed to a chair that had been added
to the circle. I told Alex I had no problem sitting on the floor
with everyone else and that I actually preferred it. He said
he assumed that would be the case but had not wanted to

embarrass me, as sitting on the floor was a problem for many Westerners. Alex instructed his wife in Arabic to remove the chair and replace it with several cushions.

Once all the introductions and arrangements had been dealt with the women joined the circle and the salads were passed around. Since I could not talk to anyone else Alex took over the conversation and gave me some background in Russian about the village and about Yasmin's family. And then his son piped up, to my surprise, in passable English. "I have seen you before, madam. I was a pupil of your friend Reverend Schick at the Gobat school and I remember you visiting there to teach him English. I must say you did an excellent job. His English improved greatly when he studied with you."

I returned the young man's compliment by saying that his English was also quite good.

"Oh, thank you, madam. My father has made sure I get the best education it is possible to get in this area. Some of my brothers have preferred to learn Russian but I think English is much more important and so I have put my efforts into learning it. I have a dream to visit your wonderful country as soon as I can."

With a lot of smiles and goodwill, we all managed to get through the meal. A sheep had been slaughtered in my honor and was placed in the middle of the table on a tray couched in a bed of rice and humus grains. It had been stabbed with cloves, which Alex explained soaked out some of the flavor of the sheep's fat. Everyone ate with gusto.

After the meal, while we were sipping our Turkish coffee, Ahmed started asking me questions about the United States and life there and what I thought about the recent assassination of my president, Abraham Lincoln. This last bit of news hit me like a physical blow. I tried to get information out of him rather than supplying him with any. I didn't realize how much I had been cut off from the outside world in the past six months.

Since Alex did not understand our conversation, he was taken aback to see my reaction to his son's words. Ahmed quickly filled his father in on the conversation. Alex answered him roughly and then invited me to come and sit with him outside under the grapevines.

"I'm so sorry my son has upset you," he said. "You must not worry yourself with these matters now. You need time to recover from your terrible ordeal. Let us talk about more pleasant things. Do you remember how we used to sit for hours together in the woods and talk about everything under the sun?"

"I have never forgotten it. It was one of the happiest periods in my life. But tell me, Alex, how did you end up here?" I asked him, and he went on to explain.

"After you left, I continued wandering around doing odd jobs. One day I took refuge in a Russian Orthodox church. The priest there pitied me and took me in to help out, cleaning the church, working on the grounds. I began to attend services and became quite religious for a while. During that time, a group of pilgrims was being organized to go to the Holy Land for Easter. I begged the priest to allow me to join them and he agreed.

"It was a very moving experience for me. We stayed in tents outside the city walls. Every day women from the surrounding villages brought us food. That is how I met Yasmin. Even though at the time we had no common language, we soon fell in love and married, and we came to live here in her village. I worked as a gardener and handyman, as I have all my life. When they opened the Russian Compound a few years ago, I got a job there."

"You seem to have quite a good life here," I said.

"It is satisfactory, but I don't really feel my religious dreams have been fulfilled and I have never quite gotten used to these unfamiliar surroundings. Life here is so difficult. One must be careful not to antagonize anyone, as you have so recently discovered for yourself."

"That is true, Alex. But despite the insecurity of life here I feel that I belong. I have no explanation for it. Believe me, I have searched for one ever since I arrived."

"I know what you're talking about. At one point I said to myself that if I had not married an Arab woman I would pick up and go back to Russia. But I am not so sure that is true either."

We sat quietly for a while, contemplating the barren Jerusalem hills.

Then suddenly I blurted out, "I have not been entirely truthful with you, Alex. But perhaps that is because I have not been entirely truthful with myself. Somewhere within me I know that I came here to find you. I could not put to rest the romantic dreams of my childhood without seeing you."

He suddenly jumped up and moved away from me to sit on a rock. "Zara, you know –"

"It's all right, Alex. Let me finish. Now that I have seen you and the life you have built for yourself, I can put those dreams to rest. I hope we'll see each other from time to time. I'll make an effort to learn more Arabic so I can communicate with your wife and children as well. But now I believe I'll be able to carve out a new corner in this world for myself as you have done."

"I'm sure you will, Zara. You are a woman of great warmth. You already have so many friends and family who care so deeply for you. And you are a very handsome woman. But I, too, am glad we had a chance to meet again and close this chapter in our lives."

"I don't know how I'll ever be able to show my gratitude for all you've done for me."

"There is no need. Believe me, the support and friendship you gave me when I was traveling around Russia as a teenager, so lonely, so frightened, has sustained me all these years. It is I who should be grateful to you. Now let us go back in and join the others."

And so my visit to Alex and his family ended. I'm sure our paths will cross in the future, but it will be different. And that is fine with me.

PART V

Chapter 27

Rebecca Continues Her Research

Spring arrived and Rebecca was making progress on her research for the Zara Rubens exhibit. From time to time Oren accompanied her on her walks around the city.

On Easter Saturday, they attended the Holy Fire Ceremony, still being celebrated every year at the Holy Sepulcher. It wasn't easy to get permission to enter the church, as pilgrims still came there by the thousands, but Oren managed to get them in through his connections with the municipality. The ceremony was not as eventful as the one Zara had attended, although the atmosphere did become electric when the flame was brought out of the aedicule. There were moments when Rebecca found the crowds and their enthusiasm almost as overwhelming as Zara had. She and Oren dodged a few overenthusiastic African pilgrims dancing around the church in ecstasy with their lit candles. One of the Africans fainted and had to be carried out on a stretcher. A new exit had been added to the building several years earlier so the fear of being stampeded to death in case of fire had greatly diminished. And, although relations between the different religious groups were still hostile, there had been no real violence during the ceremony for years.

Later they walked past the house that Oren thought Zara must have rented in the Moslem Quarter, but they didn't get up the courage to knock on the door. "Perhaps another time," Oren pointed out. "They aren't really comfortable these days with stories about Jews living in their homes."

They turned back to the Christian Quarter Road, passing near the shop where Moses Shapira had sold his artifacts. They then made their way through the Armenian Quarter to Bishop Gobat's school, where Zara had spent time recovering from her incarceration. They discovered that it was now the Jerusalem University College, a place where young Christians come to learn about the Holy Land. Behind the college was the nineteenth-century Protestant cemetery where Gobat and Conrad Schick were buried, along with several other Christian personages of the period.

They sat in the shade of a tree by Conrad's grave for a while. On the large gray headstone were written the dates of Conrad's lifespan, 1822–1901, along with those of his wife Friederike, who had been buried alongside him a year after his death. This was the first time Rebecca felt a tangible connection to Zara's old friend. She took photographs for her exhibit.

"What a long, rich life he lived. What things he must have seen. And it's certainly fortunate he was a part of Zara's life."

Oren agreed. "And of many others. We've learned a lot about those times from him and he's given a lot to the city."

After sitting for a while and enjoying the breathtaking view, Oren and Rebecca strolled down the winding path from Mount Zion and through the Hinnom Valley, in the direction of Hebron Road. They stopped along the way at the Jerusalem Cinematheque restaurant for some refreshment. The place was buzzing with activity, abruptly pulling them out of the slower-paced nineteenth century.

Chapter 28

Zara Falls in Love

October 1865

I remained at the Gobat school for a few more weeks until I began to sense I was overstaying my welcome. When I felt strong enough, I moved back to my home in the Moslem Quarter. That is when the loneliness and depression hit me. Carrie was still needed in England and will probably not be back for months, if ever at all, so I had no one to talk to.

Especially after the visit to Alex, a gaping emptiness replaced the warm feeling I had experienced on finding him again and I became restless. Thoughts of leaving the country crossed my mind, which hasn't happened for a long time now. My life had been quite pleasant for a while and I had felt, if not at home, at least that I had a small niche of my own in this nest of intrigue and peril. Now, having personally experienced some of that peril, the much-safer life in America was beginning to look more attractive. All the guilt feelings I felt about my family came up again and I vowed I would return to America at least for a visit before I died.

To keep my mind occupied I decided to start writing again. Religious subjects are taboo so I looked around for something hopefully less controversial. I've been walking around on my own, even though I'm constantly warned how dangerous it is. My life-threatening experience seems to have had the opposite effect on me than it should have. I feel invincible.

One morning last week, I decided to go over to the first neighborhood built outside the walls of the city by Sir Moses

Montefiore, the man James had spoken of so highly when I first arrived in Jerusalem. He has fulfilled his promise to build a place for Jews to live and work. During his 1855 visit, he bought a piece of land across from Mount Zion. The area came to be known as Mishkenot Sha'ananim, Hebrew for "tranquil dwellings." As far as Jerusalem is concerned, this name can only be wishful thinking.

Montefiore's first plan had been to build a hospital on the site but it was not realized, as patients feared the dangers in the "wilderness" outside the walls. In the end, he decided to construct residential housing, as well as a windmill, of all things. He hoped the mill would supply flour at a lower price than that exacted by the Arab millers, helping to ease the plight of the poor Jews. All the construction equipment was sent to Jerusalem from London. At first the mill was operated by millers from Canterbury, but later it was leased to a local Jew.

There are more than twenty modest houses. The original idea had been that people would live in them for three years at a time and then make way for another group. In reality, it was only with difficulty that enough families could be persuaded to occupy the homes in the first place. People were afraid to be separated from the rest of the Jewish community at night. In the end, it was decided to give the homes permanently to those who were brave enough to live there. They were provided with seeds and garden tools to tempt them to stay. Someone told me that a few of the tenants are fraudulently taking the money and only spending a few hours a day in the new neighborhood.

Because of the strict hygiene rules there, the inhabitants have managed to avoid catching various diseases that prevail inside the city. This, I suspect, should make the area more appealing in future.

I wandered around trying to get a feel for the neighborhood. Several gardens are well tended but there was almost no one to be seen. After a while, I met a modern, well-dressed Jew who had come over recently from England to help out with Montefiore's project. He admitted to having been smitten by the romance of the city, as so many of us have been. We got to talking and decided to share a meal at a hotel inside the walls.

His name is Ben Cohen. He also emigrated as a child from Russia, but to England. He has been married and widowed and has two grown, married daughters in London. He explained that he came over here because he believed in Montefiore's dream of a future home for Jews here and, although it wouldn't come about in his lifetime, he hoped his grandchildren might benefit from it.

We liked each other immediately and spent all afternoon and evening walking and talking. I took him to some of the shops Carrie and I had frequented. I bought him an authentic tarbush, which he cheerfully wore during our perambulations, its tassel bobbing from side to side as he gesticulated enthusiastically. I don't know if he was aware how ridiculous he really looked or that he was causing a few raised eyebrows among the authentic tarbush wearers, but I had no intention of pointing this out to him. It was great to spend time again with someone who had a sense of humor and enjoyed life.

We agreed to meet the next day for lunch and from that day on we have been inseparable. We spend hours together, walking around the city and the surrounding area. We share the experiences of our lives till now. We have discovered a lot of common beliefs, common experiences, common joys and common sorrows.

Chapter 29

Meeting with Holman-Hunt

An excerpt from a letter to Helga, 1865:

...Helga, I have wonderful news for you. It has been two months now since Ben and I met, and last night we decided to get married. I have never known such happiness, such peace. From the beginning being with him has felt so natural. We enjoy each other's company immensely. When we get tired of walking around, we go to the Arab coffee houses where I used to sit on my own from time to time. We spend hours over a plate of humus and a cup of coffee, watching the locals indulge in their favorite pastimes – puffing on their hookahs, playing chess or shesh besh while fondling their prayer beads, which they count out absentmindedly as if flicking through a pile of bills. We read month-old newspapers and exchange a few words from time to time in subdued tones.

We laughed together recently over the reminiscences of the writer Mark Twain about his voyage to the Holy Land. I thank you for sending on the resulting articles to me. I certainly have enjoyed them.

Twain's account of his visit here, although far from complimentary, is refreshing in a way. Many of his contemporaries have used their firsthand encounters and disappointments with the realities of the Holy Land to displace the actual biblical land with the American New Jerusalem. Twain, on the other hand, was just having some sacrilegious fun, and financing his trip around the world at the same time. There is no doubt much to parody here.

When Ben and I have had enough of café sitting, we choose a location and go for an outing. The places we choose are not always the safest, we know, but Ben feels as invincible as I do now that we have each other. There is never a time when we do not have some amazing experience or come across some eccentric or unusual character.

Am enclosing a copy of the article I sent in to the Times on one of the most interesting people we came across, William Holman-Hunt. After the fascinating afternoon we spent with him he invited us to visit him in his home on the Street of the Prophets in Jerusalem, promising to regale us with more of his adventures. Ben and I said we would be pleased to visit him. I asked him if he was acquainted with Wilhelm Shapira, as I knew Wilhelm now lived in a house not far from there. He said he had made the man's acquaintance but preferred to keep his distance from him and his questionable affairs....

AN AFTERNOON WITH WILLIAM HOLMAN-HUNT
Jerusalem, November 1865

One morning, a friend and I decided to set off for Bethlehem on foot. As often happens on our walks, we never made it to Bethlehem. Along the way we stopped at the Greek Orthodox monastery of Mar Elias, which stands staunchly along the road like an unassailable fortress.

In front of the monastery a man was sitting painting, deep in concentration. He had a long, free-flowing beard and shoulder-length, dusty hair topped with a peaked cap. Around his waist was a thick belt with a large revolver hanging down his left thigh and for further protection, or perhaps just for show, a shotgun was leaning against his knee.

He turned out to be British, and we began conversing. We soon learned he was the painter William Holman-Hunt. When he discovered that my friend was British and I was American he put down his brushes and offered us some of the cheese, bread, olives and wine he had brought along for the day and began telling us about his experiences in the country.

He first came to Jerusalem in 1854 at the age of twenty-seven with the British landscape painter Thomas Seddon. He worked for a while on a painting called *Christ in the Temple* but had great difficulty finding models and soon ran out of money.

While studying Jewish history for the Temple picture, he became interested in the ancient Jewish ceremony of Azazel, in which a goat is driven into the wilderness to expiate believers of their sins, what most people call "the scapegoat." Aside from his fascination with the subject, he had very practical reasons for this choice. He figured a goat would be easier to find as a model than a man.

He then put into action his plan to do this painting. It was easy to see that Hunt's zealousness far exceeded any sensible considerations. Everything he did was taken to the extreme. His first decision was that the goat had to be white. As for the location for the painting, though there were many remarkable settings around the city he could use, he searched out the most menacing area imaginable, which turned out to be the desolate desert of the Dead Sea. He could not be deterred by the warnings of the consul and others about the obstacles to such a journey: the harsh climate conditions, the great expense and, first and foremost, the grave dangers a foreigner faced traveling in an area known for its fierce tribal conflicts.

It was difficult to find people to accompany him into this region. In the end, he finally managed to collect a small group of pitiful misfits. From the beginning they were continually attacked by savage ruffians trying to steal their equipment and weapons. He said his personal bodyguard spent most of the time quaking with fear. And, of course, he had chosen to travel in November, when they were forced to battle heavy rain and thunderstorms with especially strong winds that hurled down large branches and boulders from the rock face above.

The frail mules he had acquired for the journey were incapable of maneuvering the tough terrain. The expedition soon got lost and ran out of food. Hunt's disheartened servant implored him to turn back but he refused.

Eventually the group managed to reach the Dead Sea. The consul had warned Hunt that he must secure the protection of the local sheik if he wanted to come out of this adventure alive. He had given Hunt a scarlet cloak to put around the sheik's shoulders when he met him and told him to recite certain prescribed messages and compliments in Arabic while doing so. When Hunt eventually encountered the sheik he said he was so filthy he could not even consider embracing him as the consul had recommended he do, so he just handed him the cloak. Hunt chuckled at the memory of this scene. The sheik grabbed the cloak, rolled it up and sat on it. With much effort, Hunt bargained the sheik down for protection and food from five hundred English pounds to a mere three.

Hunt's main concern, however, was the safety of the white goat. On the way, it either walked or was carried by disgruntled porters. At night it regularly snuck into Hunt's tent looking for food. It was constantly being bitten by poisonous insects. Wild animals circled close by, waiting for it to finally give up the ghost, which in due time it did. Undaunted, Hunt continued down to the Dead Sea to the constant grumblings of his entourage, where he managed to at least complete the background for the painting.

Back in Jerusalem, he made efforts to find another white goat but it turned out that he could only get one from a long distance away. The first one, brought to him from beyond the Jordan, died a day after its arrival and he had to send out for another. To make a very long story short, the picture finally got finished the following year. ◆

Chapter 30

James Finn Dies in Wimbledon

On board ship back to Palestine, 1872
I write in my journal much less these days. Life is too full to take time out. But a very tragic event has occurred. James Finn has died. Since their return to England, James had not been healthy, and it was only a matter of time before I received this announcement. Since Ben had been planning for ages to take a trip home and deal with his affairs, I went with him to visit my dear friend Elizabeth in Wimbledon.

Elizabeth, although of course very sad, is holding her own, as could only be expected from a woman whose faith is so deep and strong. She is busy writing books and editing James's remaining notes. She also collects funds to support Kerem Avraham.

It was wonderful to meet up with her again. We had a lot to catch up on. On parting we reassured each other that somehow life would bring us together once more, although I have my doubts that will happen.

The trip was also an excellent opportunity for me to get to know Ben's daughters and their husbands. They seemed a loving family and were very receptive to me. But they made me miss my own even more. I decided to continue on to America.

Before I sailed I went to see Carrie, who had been in London for quite a while. She has a romantic little flat in a rural area far away from the bustle of the city. As always, it was wonderful to be with her. We gossiped about our mutual friends and acquaintances in Jerusalem and I of course told her about my marriage to Ben. She was happy for me and admitted to having become involved herself with a local diplomat. She was following him off to India.

She then went on to a subject I found a bit awkward. "I have been meaning to talk with you about something and this seems to be the perfect opportunity," she said. "I don't know if you have been informed, but I had a visit from an American who called himself Mr. Saunders a while ago. He has recruited me to work for the Americans in India."

"Is he connected to the Times?" I asked.

"Oh, come on, Zara. Don't be so coy. You really are a dark horse."

I hesitated for a minute and then decided to keep my counsel. I told her I had no idea what she was talking about and went on to chatter about my impending visit to my family. I'm sure I was not that convincing. Perhaps someday we'll be able to talk more freely on this subject. It was of course difficult to say goodbye. Clearly, Carrie won't be coming back to Palestine for quite a while either, if at all.

Arriving in New York was a curative experience. Unlike the first time I entered the country, this time I was given the royal treatment by the authorities, thanks to my New York Times credentials and the apparently not-insignificant renown I have acquired from my articles. I considered this retribution for the humiliation my family had suffered when we first arrived.

But I did not dwell on that for long. As soon as I got through immigration, there were the boys and their families awaiting me with open arms and a huge bouquet of flowers, more flowers than I had seen in the last sixteen years. The tears did not stop the entire two weeks I spent with them. They seemed contented with their lives and their children seemed well on their way to acquiring even more prestigious professions than their parents had. They did not lack for anything.

Each of the boys took me aside to convince me to give up this nonsense of living in Jerusalem and return to the bosom of my family. For a short time, I was tempted. I looked in the mirror and saw a woman much altered from the one who had left so long ago. My hair is so gray and not very fashionable because I wear it loose most of the time. I'm much thinner than I was then and my face is lined and drawn, partially thanks to the time I spent as a guest of the Russians. My intense lifestyle has certainly taken its toll. If it weren't for the fact that Ben was waiting for me on the other side of the Atlantic, and that my life in Jerusalem was much more attractive to me than what New York had to offer a matron of my years, I might have accepted their offer.

I went into the Times to meet the people who had been so encouraging and supportive over the years and signed a new contract. The place has developed a lot since I visited it years ago with Helga. They were in the process of installing electricity, which will make putting out the newspaper much more efficient. The editor informed me that the State Department had requested I pay them a visit while I was on the continent. He assumed it had something to do with getting diplomatic cover for my writing. I thanked him and said I would take care of it.

Then there was the visit to Helga. When she opened the door, I was dumbstruck. Unlike me, she looked almost as zestful as the woman I had left so many years before. We hugged warmly. There seemed to be a note of concern in her voice, though. I guess I must have changed even more than she had expected.

The apartment looked more or less the same, except for the added litter of sixteen more years of hoarding. I noticed all of Karl's books were still sitting on the shelves where they had been all the years I had visited there. We jumped right into talking about everything – my life in Jerusalem, hers in New York, how the world had changed in the short span of our lives.

Helga listened a lot more than she used to. "How different you are, Zara," she said to me. "You've become so confident, so free."

We talked into the night. She told me about Karl, who had died of cancer a few years earlier, and about their son Nathan, who still lives in Boston. Much of what we had to say we had written in our correspondence and in our articles, exchanged regularly through the mail, but we were able to fill in some of the more piquant details which one doesn't always like to commit to paper – especially my stories about my incarceration in the Russian Compound.

"So, tell me, my dear," Helga asked before I left. "Do you now know why you're living there?"

"To tell you the truth, Helga, I don't, but it doesn't really matter because I don't think I could live anywhere else now. That is my world. You must come one day and see. I'm sure you'd never leave either."

We hugged again and I left.

Chapter 31

The American Colony

An excerpt from a letter to Helga, 1873:

...Ben and I are now living in the Nahalat Shiva area completed only a few years ago. The name means "Inheritance of the Seven" because it was built by seven Jews from the Old City. We decided to leave our home in the Moslem Quarter due to the recent cholera epidemic and the overcrowding, which brought our landlord to raise our rent by a prohibitive amount.

Ben has become friendly with Joseph Rivlin, one of the founders of the Nahalat Shiva project, and is now working with him on another new neighborhood called Mea Shearim, which was originally designed by Conrad about ten years before I arrived. Conrad has now become one of the main architectural designers of the city. He is also building a home for himself and his family not far from Wilhelm's home and the Russian Compound.

I have made the acquaintance of a remarkable family that has moved to Jerusalem under very tragic circumstances. Their names are Horatio and Anna Spafford.

They have had a very difficult life in Chicago, including several painful personal and financial losses. They came here to escape the persecution of the Presbyterian Church, which refused to accept their religious views. They were joined by fourteen other people who shared their beliefs.

After touring the country – the men in heavy business suits, the women in long, full skirts, tight waists, and fitted blouses – they moved into their first rented house in the Moslem Quarter.

They are now setting up a community of their own and seem very industrious and serious. It's called the American Colony. The colony members are teaching local mothers how to care for their children, running English and Bible classes, advising farmers on how to improve their crops and caring for numerous visitors who come to stay. Horatio has sent for seeds from abroad and is planting the first potatoes and eucalyptus trees in the Holy Land, a welcome addition to the barren landscape.

I do what I can to familiarize them with daily life in the city and invite Anna and Horatio to our new home outside the walls for dinner from time to time. They have become fast friends with Eliezer Ben-Yehuda and his wife Dvora, who settled in Jerusalem a month after they did. Eliezer and Horatio both teach at the recently opened Alliance Israélite School for Jewish boys. Horatio gives free English classes and Ben-Yehuda teaches Hebrew for very little money. Ben-Yehuda's mission in life is to revive Hebrew as the spoken language of the Jews in Palestine.

I find myself attracted to the Spaffords' charity work. I remember the promise I made Miss Cooper all those years ago that when I settled in I would help. So I've decided the time has come to do so. I teach some English but mostly I work in the hospital they are setting up to care for the misfortunate of the city. I feel I am doing penance for all the other activities I have been involved in, which sit less and less well with my conscience these days....

Chapter 32

A Letter from Elizabeth

An excerpt from a letter from Elizabeth, April 1884:

Dear Zara,

The years pass and I often think back to our time in Jerusalem. James and I tried to make a difference and I hope that in some way we did. I also think of you and am pleased you have built a life for yourself. Ben is a good man. I read your articles in the New York Times and learn a lot from them.

Although you have probably heard the brouhaha over there, I thought I'd fill you in as to what has been happening with our old friend – if he ever was a friend – Moses Shapira. I am so troubled as to how this fellow lost his way despite Conrad's efforts and those of so many others. I blame that scoundrel Selim al-Khouri.

As you might have heard, Moses arrived here last summer with what has become known as the Shapira strips, fifteen leather strips he claimed are fragments of a scroll of Deuteronomy. He tried to sell them to the British Museum, with whom he'd been dealing for years, for a million pounds sterling. Two of the strips were exhibited while the rest were being examined by a prominent biblical scholar.

The French scholar Clermont-Ganneau got wind of the matter and arrived in London to investigate the strips. He had previously proved that the Moabite pottery Shapira had sold to the German government were forgeries. He even found the workshop where the pottery had been made, which not surprisingly belonged to Selim al-Khouri. Whether Shapira was duped by Selim or was a party to the forgery remains uncertain.

The day after the Deuteronomy manuscript was declared a forgery, Shapira wrote to the museum: "[Y]ou have made a fool of me by publishing and exhibiting them [the fragments], that you believe them to be false. I do not think that I will be able to survive this shame. Although I am not yet convinced the ms. is a forgery, unless M. Ganneau did it. I will leave London in a day or two for Berlin."

Shapira then disappeared for more than six months. And last month I am sorry to say he committed suicide in a Rotterdam hotel. May his soul rest in peace....

PART VI

Chapter 33

Rebecca Discovers Zara's Secret

Rebecca was fascinated by the journals about the American Colony and began doing research on the subject. She still felt that the full story of Zara's life in Jerusalem had not yet come to light.

Rebecca had recently shared her thoughts with Oren. "I always have the feeling there were things going on in Zara's life she never disclosed in her journals, her letters and her articles. She was too involved in the life of the city, she knew too many people, she had access to too much information for an American matron in no official capacity."

"Keep digging, Beck. I'm sure you'll find something. I've learned to trust your instincts."

The next day Rebecca visited an exhibition on the history of the American Colony at the hotel of that name, which had been converted from the residence of the original settlement. The photographs, documents and artifacts exhibited were drawn from the archives of a Mrs. Valentine Vester.

Rebecca went up to the desk to find out more about Mrs. Vester. The clerk explained. "Mrs. Vester lives in the hotel but is quite old and we don't like to disturb her."

"Perhaps you might try to get her permission to allow me just a few minutes of her time. Please tell her I'm the great-grandniece of an old friend of Anna Spafford named Zara Rubens."

The clerk didn't seem to be overly surprised by Rebecca's request; apparently, it was a common occurrence. After a short phone conversation, he asked Rebecca to follow him through the winding halls of the hotel to her quarters.

The door was opened by a nurse. She led Rebecca into the high-ceilinged sitting room of a rather spacious apartment. The lighting was unusually bright. She offered her an armchair, next to which sat a microphone. "Speak clearly, dear," the nurse requested politely. She then introduced Rebecca to a withered, but very alert, woman in her nineties, who was sitting rigidly on a sofa a few feet away in a long-sleeved, gray cotton dress, her shoulders swathed in a maroon-colored woolen scarf.

"I hope you are well, Mrs. Vester," Rebecca said carefully into the microphone.

"Aside from the fact that I can hardly see, hear or walk there is nothing wrong with me. I am quite well, thank you."

She then proceeded to speak freely about herself. She was born in Yorkshire, England, married into the Spafford family and arrived in Jerusalem in 1963, when her husband, Horatio, a British lawyer and Spafford heir, took over the failing hotel.

"Back then we did all the work ourselves," she said. "I was in charge of the kitchen and most of the gardening around the hotel."

Rebecca eventually brought the conversation around to Mrs. Vester's husband's grandmother and asked her if she had heard or read about Zara Rubens.

"Of course I have. Your aunt was a dear friend of Anna's. Anna's daughter, Bertha, remembered her fondly from childhood."

Rebecca explained that she was preparing an exhibit on Zara and wondered if there was anything Mrs. Vester could contribute.

"Well, when we prepared *our* exhibit I reread Anna's journals and I remember several references to Zara. As you may or may not know, relations between the American Colony and the American Consulate were very tense for years. Zara used her not inconsiderable influence at the consulate to smooth things over more than once."

"What do you mean by her influence?"

The old lady hesitated for a minute and then said. "Oh, my dear, you still have a lot to learn about your relative. Zara was much more than the matronly journalist she presented herself to be."

"I beg your pardon."

"Well, to put it bluntly, young lady, your aunt was what you might call – a spy."

"What?" Rebecca dropped her notebook and quickly bent down to pick it up again, not wanting to miss a word of what the woman had to say.

"Yes, dear, under the cover of being a journalist she provided extensive information of what was going on in this country to the American government. As complex as things are now politically, there was an enormous amount of intrigue going on back then as well. The British, Americans, Germans and Russians were all trying to grab as much land as they could. This required the establishment of a well-oiled espionage system. Everyone was doing it."

Rebecca sat openmouthed. Finally, she stammered, "But why has this never come out?"

"Nobody has ever bothered to delve into the story. If you like, you can have a look at some of Anna's journals. I assure you they will shed a good deal of light on the subject for you."

After they conversed for a while longer, Mrs. Vester arranged for Rebecca to sit in a small study in the back of the hotel. An assistant brought in the relevant journals. Waiters unobtrusively arrived with lunch and later dinner. Rebecca read late into the evening.

As Mrs. Vester had said, there were several references to Zara in Anna's journals. In fact, she had devoted a whole section to Zara's imprisonment. Rebecca learned that Zara had been questioned regularly during the time she was held in the Russian Compound – not about her article but more about her other activities. The American Consulate refrained from intervening because they weren't exactly aware of what the Russians knew – a feeble excuse, thought Rebecca – but they did provide Conrad with assistance to get her out and support her afterwards.

Rebecca left the hotel deep in thought, almost getting run over by a car entering the hotel's circular driveway. She decided it would be best to take a taxi home.

The next day she called the American Embassy in Tel Aviv to make an appointment with someone who could tell her about Zara's other career. Again, the fact that she was doing an exhibit at the Israel Museum won her an interview the following morning.

She was ushered into the office of a bland-looking official who offered her a cup of coffee and, in typical American fashion, came straight to the point. "This is the information we have on your aunt," he said, patting a file on his desk. "Since none of it is classified anymore I see no reason why you should not take a copy of it with you."

And without further ado he handed her a thick file labeled "Zara Rubens, 1863–1883." Just like that.

She began to read through it voraciously on the bus back to Jerusalem. The first thing she read was a form Zara had filled out when beginning her work for the Americans. In answer to the question "Why do you want to do this job?" her response had been, "The United States has given my family the opportunity to live a comfortable and satisfying life. I feel I owe the country something in exchange."

From the rest of the file Rebecca learned that Zara's espionage activities began when she was asked to provide information on the Artas affair and continued all through her years in the country until she reached the age of seventy. She had had mixed feelings writing about her friends and acquaintances, but from the reports of the officials she communicated with, it was evident she had done so with discretion and sensitivity.

Chapter 34

Sad News

Jerusalem, September 25, 1890

Dearest Helga,

It has been ages since we corresponded and it is unfortunate that this first communication after such a long time bears such melancholy news.

It is my sad duty to inform you that our remarkable friend, Zara Rubens, is no more. She fell ill suddenly, and despite all efforts by her friends to provide her with the best possible care, she died peacefully in her sleep at the hospital run by her friend Anna Spafford. Ben's death last year, I am afraid, took the spirit out of her completely. She has never been the same since. I decided to return to Jerusalem one last time to collect her personal effects and send them on to her family in America. As I have had no contact with them for years, I am entrusting these belongings to you in the hope you'll find a way to pass them on.

I've included a few of my letters as well.

Please convey my condolences to her children and grandchildren. Tell them their mother and grandmother was an amazing woman, a talented writer, a compassionate and loyal friend, and in her final years a saintly nurturer of the ill and suffering. I have also discovered of late that beyond all this she was a stalwart American patriot. Tell them the journals, pictures and articles enclosed tell only a fraction of the story.

I will miss her sorely, as I am sure you will too. May God rest her soul!

With fondest regards,
Elizabeth Finn

EPILOGUE

Chapter 35

The Exhibit

Rebecca mingled among the guests. She was glad Oren had convinced her to do the exhibit at Ticho House instead of at the main museum. The massive stone walls of the Arab building were more suited to the subject of the exhibit than the modern structure of the Givat Ram museum.

The location also gave the exhibit a more intimate feel, especially since it was physically closer in a way to several of the figures it presented. It was fitting that the Russian Compound was close by and that Conrad Schick had once lived across the road. She was glad she had managed to get on loan two of Schick's famous wooden models to display in the exhibit. It was perhaps less satisfying that Moses Shapira had lived in this exact building.

Rebecca had been so immersed in Zara's life for so long now that seeing it spread out before her, being pried into by strangers, felt like an intrusion into her own private life. She looked around at the familiar faces of those she had spent hours talking to about Zara, the people Zara had known and the life she had lived. She felt like Zara was there among them.

She was relieved that the representative of the Russian Church had reacted positively to the exhibit, as she had made a particular effort not to offend the church when preparing that chapter in Zara's story. And she didn't think she was imagining it when the American consul gave her a conspiratorial wink when he approached her.

Out of the corner of her eye, she also noticed the American great-great-grandchildren of Alex, Zara's childhood love, conversing with the representative of the Swedish Theological Seminary, who had been so helpful in showing her around Conrad's home. Alex's son, Ahmed, had fulfilled his dream and gone off to live in America. Zara had helped him establish himself in New York by getting him a clerical job at the *Times*. Although the family had moved out west later on, it hadn't been that hard to track down Ahmed's descendants. They had been emailing back and forth for months now. She was very pleased when they agreed to accept her invitation to come to the opening.

She continued upstairs to the rest of the exhibit. She saw Anna Spafford's granddaughter conscientiously reading from the journal pages displayed under glass. She kept her distance, not wanting to spoil the experience. Rebecca had chosen carefully the pages she thought Zara would be willing to share with the world. Aside from their political sensitivity, there were several she felt were too private to expose.

Reading Zara's final journals had been the most poignant part of this whole experience. In her old age, Zara had poured out on paper many of the regrets she had had. She could not excuse herself for the information she had passed on to the Americans about the Finns, although she knew they could have gotten to it in a number of different ways. Nevertheless, she still felt partially responsible for James losing his post. She had also dedicated several pages to the Russian Compound incident, berating herself endlessly for endangering so many people because of her own arrogance. And, of course, she never forgave herself for having missed all those years of her grandchildren's lives.

Rebecca promised herself she would learn from Zara's experience and do her best not to have any more regrets than those she already had, though she knew that was impossible. She also realized that her tie to her Jewish roots here in Israel had nothing to do with religion but was more of a historical, ethnic one. She was now sure that she wanted to learn more about this country today and find her place in it.

Oren came over and offered her a glass of wine. "You must be so proud, Rebecca. It's an excellent exhibit. Not only have you presented Zara's life story but it's a picture of the whole period."

"Why, thank you, Mr. Curator. But I think you're right. Who would have believed a year ago that I would be standing here receiving congratulations from all these dignitaries. It's been a long journey. I feel like I've crammed into a year what Zara experienced over thirty-five years. I've also learned a lot about myself and who I am. It's incredible. But I couldn't have done it without you, my dearest," she concluded, clinking her glass appreciatively against his.

They both sipped their wine slowly, quite pleased with themselves.

"So, what now?" Oren ventured, slightly wary of the answer to come.

"Who knows? Maybe I'll start looking into your family. See what I can find."

Their exchange was interrupted by some eager tourists who had happened upon the exhibit after having dined in the ground-floor restaurant and were anxious to meet the curator.

Bibliography

Ben-Arieh, Yehoshua. *Jerusalem in the 19th Century: Emergence of the New City*. Jerusalem: Yad Izhak Ben-Zvi Press, 1986.

Ben-Arieh, Yehoshua. *Jerusalem in the 19th Century: The Old City*. Jerusalem: Yad Izhak Ben-Zvi Press, 1984.

Dudman, Helga, and Ruth Kark. *The American Colony: Scenes from a Jerusalem Saga*. Jerusalem: Carta, 1998.

Eliav, Mordechai. *Britain and the Holy Land*. Jerusalem: Yad Izhak Ben-Zvi Press, 1997.

Elon, Amos. *Jerusalem: City of Mirrors*. London: Flamingo Publishers, 1996.

Erlanger, Steven. "The Saturday Profile: A Grande Dame of a Bygone Jerusalem," *New York Times*, October 29, 2005.

Finn, James. *Stirring Times*. 2 vols. London: C. Kegan Paul & Co., 1878. Facsimile edition: London: Elibron Classics, 2005.

Goren, Haim, ed. *Conrad Schick: L'ma'an Yerushalayim* [Conrad Schick: For Jerusalem]. Jerusalem: Ariel Publishing House, 1998.

Holman-Hunt, Diana. *My Grandfather: His Wives and Loves*. London: Hamish Hamilton Ltd., 1969.

"Description of the Miracle of Holy Fire that Happens Every Year in Jerusalem," http://www.holyfire.org/eng/velich.htm.

Lagerloff, Selma. *The Holy City: Jerusalem*. Translated by Velma Swanston Howard. New York: Doubleday, Page & Company, 1918.

Lapid, Shulamit. *Ka'heres ha'nishbar* [As a Broken Vessel]. Jerusalem: Keter Publishing House, 1984.

McCaul Finn, Elizabeth A. *A Home in the Holy Land*. London: James Nisbet & Co., 1866. Fascimile edition: London: Elibron Classics, 2003.

Oz, Amos. *A Tale of Love and Darkness*. Translated by Nicholas de Lange. London: Chatto & Windus, 2004.

Reiner, Fred. "Tracking the Shapira Case: A Biblical Scandal Revisited," http://members.bib-arch.org/publication.asp?PubID=BSBA&Volume=23&Issue=03&ArticleID=02.

About the Author

Sue Kerman is a Jerusalem educator born in Winnipeg, Canada. She has lived in Jerusalem for forty-three years and has worked in English education for thirty of those years. Until recently she taught English literature at the David Yellin College in Jerusalem. She has also written over twenty EFL textbooks and readers for second-language English teaching for both local and foreign EFL publishers.